In Search of Unicorns

YOULANDA BREWSTER

In Search of Unicorns

MODERN FAIRYTALES FOR MODERN WOMEN

TATE PUBLISHING
AND ENTERPRISES, LLC

Published by Tate Publishing & Enterprises, LLC
127 E. Trade Center Terrace | Mustang, Oklahoma 73064 USA
1.888.361.9473 | www.tatepublishing.com

Tate Publishing is committed to excellence in the publishing industry. The company reflects the philosophy established by the founders, based on Psalm 68:11,
"The Lord gave the word and great was the company of those who published it."

Book design copyright © 2013 by Tate Publishing, LLC. All rights reserved.
Cover design by Arjay Grecia
Interior design by Jomel Pepito

Published in the United States of America

ISBN: 978-1-62994-868-3
1. Fiction / Short Stories (Single Author)
2. Fiction / General
13.10.08

To Mom, who dreamed a little dream
and tricked me into coming out.
I must admit, you did not lie. My
space was cramped and dark and
there was more room on the outside.
Even when we're apart, I love
to hear you smile.

Table Of Contents

Love Can Build 9

Got It Maid 35

No Greater Love...77

The First Time 86

Nappy And Me: Through The Storm 96

The Bag's... A Lady..106

Beast Of Burden...152

The Gift..179

Love Can Build

"A mass of moving bodies and he's swallowed up amongst them", she thought. As the swarm of bodies swarm the busy streets and the Old World Orient charm mixed with the modern day extravagances, she fought to keep sight of Nicholi.

A push cart vied for space with a Mercedes in the streets as Western garb passed Oriental on the sidewalk. Nicholi stood out in his American suit which was at home on his broad shoulders, his long stride was purpose-filled as he towered above most those buzzing about him.

For a moment Kali lost sight of him as she dodged in and out of the sea of bodies. She was saved from losing him only by his need to pause before crossing the street. She came to a halt beside him but not for long for a disapproving glance from an older Oriental man had her hesitantly stepping back until she was slightly behind him.

In a blink he was off again. In the rush of the day
the two were quickly separated. Kali opened her mouth
to call him but the words died unspoken. She pushed
through the ocean which appeared to swallow him up
but in vain.

She finally came to a stop at a street corner, eyes
bright with unshed tears. She sagged against the corner
of the nearest building. "Oh Nicholi..." she whispered
brokenly. A single tear fell as she turned and headed
back in the direction from which she had just fought
to come.

Kali stood before the fireplace, her eyes turned to a far
away place. She sighed deeply then refocused on the
present. She turned from the mantle and looked about
the room.

Like one aged, she moved slowly across the room to
the highly lacquered writing desk. She lightly touched
the letter which laid on the glossy top. Taking a breath,
she picked up the pen on the blotter and quickly
scrawled her name across the bottom before folding it
and slipping it in a matching envelope. Before she could
change her mind she propped it against the model of a
house which held center stage on the desk.

She then turned and moved purposely to the front
door. She came to a halt then turned and retraced her
steps. Once at the desk again, she gently slipped her
wedding rings from her finger and slid them into the
envelope. Trembling, she moved back to the door and

picked up a single suitcase. One final look back and Kali was out the door.

Six and a half years later...

Kali Donely sat watching her fellow executives about the conference table. Her expression was slightly bored. With the exception of Florenstein she was the only female present out of nine office heads, not that Florenstein Crawford had ever agreed with her on anything for fear of being called a female. Florenstein had never forgiven Kali for making it beyond the typing pool and she never would.

Kali drew her attention back to the present as the Chairman cleared his throat, an action he was fond of doing on a somewhat regular basis. "I believe this is a step forward for this company and we have Kali to thank for it. Her insight into today's market has helped us divert a coming disaster... in other words, she pretty much saved all our asses, not to mention jobs."

A murmur went around the table but Kali's expression didn't change for she knew not one there was grateful of any move she made. For in the four and a half years she had managed her own department they had all sought at one time or another to at the least discredit her and at the most, get her fired.

She was young blood and female and they made certain she knew they didn't care for either on their playing field. The ringing of the phone before him halted the Chairman's speech to Kali's relief. "Yes, give us five then send him in." He replaced the receiver. "To assist us in our expansion, Kokato Industries has lent us their best man to get the new site started."

As the door opened in less than five minutes, Kali glanced back and grew pale.

Kali concentrated on her task, meticulously washing her hands. "He is rather attractive... for an Asian." She stiffened but continued, her vision blurring slightly.

"True, but you know what they say about them—very passive and unimaginative in the bedroom."

"But what about that movie? You know, the one where the Asian man takes a young girl as a lover."

"Any man can please a young innocent, besides, it was only a movie. We're talking about the real thing."

The first woman laughed, slightly embarrassed. "I guess you're right, it's a shame though. What a waste." The two women exchanged insincere smiles and left the bathroom.

Kali ceased her pretense and closed her eyes. Her hands trembled as she took a deep breath. She stared unseeingly into the mirror.

"Your neck is wet." A soft male voice caressed her ear. Kali swung about. Nicholi gave her a knowing smile and walked away. Though her body remained across the room, her eyes followed him. Her heart let it be known that it was still there. It pounded within her as it, her mind and her body as one remembered.

A younger freer Kali raced up the stairs. Nicholi flew in hot pursuit. Both knew he could have easily caught her yet was enjoying the chase.

As she reached the door, her laughter made it impossible for her to fit the key into the lock. Nicholi soon joined her. Covering the hand holding the key with his own, he inserted it into the lock. The other hand made its way about her body and pressed its palm against her abdomen, drawing her back against him. The laughter ceased as she closed her eyes and relaxed against him with a satisfied sigh.

For a moment they stood as such. Nicholi caressed her neck with his lips using the barest of touches. Kali sighed. "I can't come in." He kissed her, "...yet". She caught her breath as he caressed her cheek. Her sigh caught in her throat as he pressed against her. "When I come, I will stay."

"Please." escaped from her yearning lips.

"In time. In time." He drew away from her warmth, his fingers caressed then released her. Kali swayed. The door opened and he gently pushed her through.

As she turned in a daze, he smiled a smile laced with promise. "Soon." She swallowed. "A little cold water at the base of the back of the neck works wonders." He drew the door to on her puzzled expression.

Self-consciously Kali wiped her neck, quickly withdrawing her hand. Her body began to shake as she looked up to see Nicholi staring from across the room. His knowing smile had her stomach tightening.

Kali's breath caught in her throat as she watched the young couple giggling before the hotel room door. She tore her eyes away as she walked past them. They didn't even acknowledge her presence just as they hadn't on the elevator ride up, their thoughts filled only of each other.

It took her two tries to find the door for which she sought and this was achieved only after the couple had backed their way into their room and closed the door. Kali laid her forehead against the door as she steadied her breathing. A soft moan escaped her tightly closed lips and she closed her eyes as though in pain for indeed she was, wrapped in the pain of the past.

A younger Nicholi and Kali sat on the sofa, papers, blueprints, charts and spec sheets were scattered on the entire surface of the coffee-table and spilled over onto the floor. Each had a yellow legal pad on their lap.

"It's gonna take work but it is possible." Kali examined her figures.

"Agreed." Nicholi responded.

Kali glanced at him in puzzlement. "So... we need a plan of attack." she prompted.

"Absolutely."

She looked at her assignment partner in frustration. "I'm so glad we're in complete agreement."

"Yes." he nodded,"Pleasant arrangement."

Her eyes narrowed. "So... you have a plan?"

"Yes."

"Would you care to share it?" she asked in exasperation.

"Of course."

For the space of a moment he was silent. Kali closed her eyes and leaned back. Nicholi allowed himself a smile which quickly disappeared as she re-opened her eyes. When she spoke, she spoke slowly as though speaking to a child. "I would like very much to know what your plans are."

Nicholi spoke just as slowly. "I know you would." He rose, leaving her wide-eyed. "Some sweet tea would be just the thing right now."

She looked about in disbelief. "Sweet tea?" She gestured to the papers. "Sweet tea?"

Nicholi walked away. "Sweet tea."

Later he re-entered with a tray holding a delicate porcelain teapot and two matching cups and saucers. He glanced up from the tray to find Kali laying on the sofa asleep, her trusty pad upside down on the carpet, her hand fallen over the edge of the chair.

Smiling, he silently crossed the room and placed his burden atop the papers on the table. He moved around the table as soundlessly as a cat.

Nicholi kneeled at the side of the chair and studied the sleeping woman. Her lips were slightly parted and he could hear the faintest whisk of her breath as it escaped. Her rich sable hair with its golden highlights, lay in soft waves about her head like a cloud. Her pale skin was a flushed and appealing peach tone. On its own accord, his hand rose and brushed feather light against the softness of her cheek.

Kali's lids fluttered like wings then slowly opened. For a moment they watched each other as the world grew still. Wordlessly he bent his head as she raised her chin for his kiss. After a time, he drew back slightly and locked her in the velvet depths of his chocolate eyes. "Your taste is so sweet and innocent." He whispered.

Kali raised her arms and wrapped them about his neck. "Have some more." She whispered.

Kali shuttered and raised her head from the door. "Why Nicholi, why did you have to come back in my life now? I was just beginning to stop missing you." She whispered. She closed her eyes briefly and mentally shook herself.

She straightened and ran a not so steady hand across her forehead. "Show-time." She muttered to herself as she knocked on the door."

"Oh God," she prayed, "help me to get out of here without making a fool of myself." Kali succeeded in stopping herself from fidgeting... barely. Yet again she jerked her eyes away from Nicholi's naked back.

"For heaven's sake it's only a back." She scolded herself but found her eyes caressing it still, for it was such a well formed back. Long and lean, his muscles rippled as he moved about the hotel room gathering the things he would need for their presentation.

Oh why had they made her his escort for the duration of his trip? Kali caught herself. But of course it made sense, the expansion had been her idea after all. Besides, the others had no way of knowing the two of them were married for she had never spoken of her private life and they only knew her by her maiden name, which she had resumed using upon her return to the states.

And Nicholi had said nothing. If only he would, she thought. It would be so much easier to handle if only she knew what he was thinking, how he felt. But she had never been able to read him she sighed.

"I'm sorry I've taken so much time." His honeyed voice broke up her thoughts.

Kali stiffened, drawing up her tattered shield of indifference. She glanced blindly at the watch on her wrist. "We have sufficient time remaining."

Nicholi chuckled, the sound dancing over her skin. "Where is my Kali I wonder, who was always so impatient for whatever life had to offer next."

Kali looked away. "She grew up almost seven years ago." She could feel his gaze going over her from the crown of her french braided hair, over the charcoal grey tailored power suit to the mid-heeled shoes on her feet. She knew he was not pleased at what he saw though his tone did not change.

"Pity." She felt when he turned away. She peeked and watched as he drew on his shirt. As he buttoned it, she stared at his well formed chest through the mirror and reminded herself to breath.

"I'll wait for you downstairs." She turned abruptly and headed for the door. In the mirror, Nicholi watched her departure and smiled.

<hr />

"Are you certain you don't wish to drive?"

Nicholi fastened his seatbelt with a decisive click. "I have other things on which to concentrate."

Kali glanced over to meet his stare. "You never cared for women driver's before."

"A lot of things have changed from before."

She turned away, "Yes they have." And some are still the same as much as I desire otherwise, she thought to herself.

The silence was broken as they sat waiting for the signal light to change. "Why?" She glanced swiftly at him then turned just as swiftly away. "Why Kali?"

I could pretend, she thought but she knew it would not fool him. "I left a letter." She opted for the truth.

"Explain."

She sighed. "Too many differences, too many rules. I needed a man I could love in public as well as private."

"You could not do this?"

"I couldn't even walk beside you much less touch you."

"The old way is..."

"Wrong, very much wrong." Her voice rose.

"And you couldn't tell me this, after two years of marriage?"

"It was your people, your country, your ways."

"I see." And he was silent.

Kali wrapped her arms about herself to halt her trembling, she did not succeed. "Why do I remember everything about him?" She asked her empty apartment. "His smile, the feel of him." She closed her eyes and leaned against the door. Tears began to flow, hot and fast. "If only I didn't remember so well." She cried as she stumbled through the living room to her bedroom.

"If only I didn't remember." She sobbed into the pillow as she fell upon the bed and curled up. "So much to remember." And she cried on.

∽⊷⊶⊷∼

The music played softly in the back ground as Kali entered from the hallway. "We should be able to catch..." She broke off in the process of putting on her jacket as she looked up to find Nicholi seated in the recliner with the seat back.

"Always sitting down on the job. Hey, we'll only be a bit late if we..." She rounded the chair and smiled. "... leave now." She ended as she stared at the sleeping young man.

She shook her head, her smile tender as she moved to the sofa and drew off the mink unicorn blanket which laid draped across the back. Quietly, she moved back to Nicholi and lovingly covered him. "Sleep well sweet prince." She whispered. As she drew back, his eyes opened and she paused in her withdrawal.

"You know I love you don't you?" He inquired, his voice husky.

"Yes." She answered in response.

"So what are you going to do about it?"

"Nothing." She bent forward and kissed him. As she began to pull away he took her by the arm and after pushing the blanket aside, drew her onto his lap.

"I thought so." He laughed as he drew her into a tighter embrace, cradling her like a child against his chest as he drew the blanket about them.

His lips were so gentle yet firm, she thought. Oh how I've missed this. She pressed closer. Kali moaned as the light pressure brushed against her throat. When the hand cupped her breast, she moaned again. The sound had her eyes opening.

"Nicholi!" She choked out. She wanted to pull away but for a moment her starving body betrayed her and that moment was all it took for him to use his weight to trap her beneath him.

She closed her eyes. "Your body remembers me, as do mine you." He spoke in her ear, and it did.

He was not fully awake yet already he knew she was gone. Slowly Nicholi stretched and opened his eyes. The first time it had not been like this.

She laid in his arms content and spent. She hummed softly as she drifted on the wings of his love. "I guess I should learn how to be a Geisha." She said after breaking off the humming.

Nicholi drew her closer in his embrace. "Had I wanted a Geisha I could have had my choice of the best. I choose you over everyone I have met or have yet to meet." And she had believed him... for a time.

Nicholi stretched again and began to hum. And shall again he thought as his lips parted in a smile.

Kali started as she felt Nicholi's arms encircling her. She stubbornly continued to stare out the window into the darkness. He pressed his face into her hair and breathed deeply, she trembled. He willed her to remember, and she did.

Kali moved to where Nicholi sat at the drafting table. She stood behind his chair savoring she didn't know which the most, the sight of him or the pralines and cream ice cream she held.

Not giving herself time to think her actions through, she swung his chair around to face her. He was not surprised. Her determination to do so grew. She gathered up her skirt and straddled his lap.

She succeeded and she smiled as she continued to eat her ice cream. When he spoke his voice was husky with just a bit of a tremble. "If you have no experience, how do you manage to wing it?"

"I use my imagination." She placed a spoon of ice cream in his mouth. Her lips parted slightly as she withdrew the now empty utensil. "And I have a very good imagination." She whispered as she leaned closer and licked the melted cream from his lips.

"How good?" He asked in a low growl. He drew her into an open mouthed kiss.

She pulled back just enough to speak. "A very vivid one."

He firmly yet gently seized her by the back of the head and deepened the kiss again. After a moment he drew back a breath. "Show me." The ice cream container and spoon fell unheeded to the floor as she did just that.

Kali sighed and Nicholi's hold tightened. "This is as it should be, man and wife together. She stiffened. "Kali?"

Abruptly she broke away. "That is the past and it will remain in the past."

"Kali."

She brushed away the sound of his voice. "I've filed for divorce, a few more days and it will be final. It only takes seven years of separation." She laughed without humor. "Funny how time flies when you start a new life."

Nicholi moved up behind her until the heat from his body wrapped itself about her, yet he did not touch her. "I know something of the law also. It will take another seven years for you to receive a divorce, we've just made certain of that."

She swung around, stumbling slightly when she bumped into him. "I'll deny ever sleeping with you!" He watched her silently. "I will!" She ran a trembling hand across her forehead. "What do you want of me?"

"Six months."

She watched him, tears of frustration in her eyes. "Six months?"

"Give me six months if you feel the same then I'll give you the divorce." Kali bowed her head.

Three months later...

Kali froze as she rounded the corner, hastily she drew back so as not to be seen. Nicholi stood half-turned to the door which was barely opened. "Suwako, I understand." She stiffened at the name. "I will let her know when it is time."

Kali hurried away to the living room. Hand trembling she quietly picked up the receiver of the phone there. "You must tell her soon Nicholi, before it comes out... such a matter..."

Nicholi interrupted. "When it is time. I know how she shall react. She will accept it, eventually... she must; therefore she shall."

"If you say you know best." The woman on the other end of the line sighed. "I hope it shall be soon so that things can be as they are meant to be once more."

"I must go Suwako."

Kali barely heard their leave taking. Hearing the dial tone jolted her, signifying the conversations end. Dazed, she replaced the receiver.

The longer she stood there the darker her mood became. In quick succession she went from deeply hurt to righteously angry. She stormed into the office. Nicholi sat sedately at the desk reviewing a file.

"Why is Suwako calling here, at my home?"

He glanced at the phone. When his eyes turned back to her, one brow was raised and a knowing look covered his face. "Is it not my home also?"

"Don't play word games with me. You made me promise you six months. Well, if you can't be faithful for three don't expect me to waste three more months out of my life."

"What do you want Kali?" He laid the file down and gave her his full attention. It made her uneasy.

"I know your family wanted... still want you to marry Suwako. So why did you come here? Why mess up my life again?" She turned away.

"Is this really how you feel, that I've only come to mess up your life?"

She swung back to face him. "Tell me I'm wrong, that you're not still seeing her. Just tell me I'm wrong!"

Slowly he rose and moved around the desk. Silently he made his way to the door. "Tell me I'm wrong!" She yelled as tears filled her eyes and overflowed.

He stopped and faced her. "You will believe what your mind chooses. Not what my words say."

She stepped towards him, her eyes pleading. "Just tell me I'm wrong." He turned back to the door. "Damn you... please!"

He shook his head sadly. "No matter what I say or don't, you have already judged. I only wait for sentencing."

Kali was shocked, acknowledging however unwilling that his words were true. His eyes sad, he walked out the room. Kali stumbled to the sofa, once there she flopped down and began to cry pitifully. Moments later the distinctive sound of the front door closing could be heard, the sound was very final.

Seven months later...

Kali rose and her companion followed suit, allowing her to pass him as she made her way to the restroom. Eyes followed her unhurried progress through the restaurant.

As Kali stood washing her hands, she felt a presence behind her. Slowly raising her head, her eyes meet Suwako's in the mirror before her. Swiftly she turned, splashing water. Instinctively she grabbed her stomach as though to protect the baby growing within. Suwako eyed her silently and smiled then walked out without a word.

Weak from the non-verbal encounter, she leaned against the counter with her eyes closed. Hand trembling, she raised it to her forehead, not noticing the water still clinging to it.

Opening her eyes finally, she drew back her hand and noted the water almost indifferently.

Kali tossed restlessly, causing the covers to wrap about her body like coils. Face bathed in perspiration, her eyes snapped open and she sat up abruptly. She covered her mouth, her expression one of horror. She began to moan, wrapping one arm about her middle.

"No, no!" She whispered as she rocked back and forth. "No, no... no." In a panic she untangled herself and threw her legs over the side of the bed. Pushing back the soaked hair sticking to her forehead she rose to her feet trembling.

"I won't let you." She spoke out to the empty room. Eyes wild, she ran to the dresser and began randomly pulling things from its drawers.

As her fear mounted she rushed to the closet. Once there she reached for the suitcase on the shelf. Unable to reach it, she began to cry. Looking wildly about she wrapped her arms about herself as her sobs shook her frame.

Suddenly her gaze lighted on a wooden crate holding files. She quickly stooped and dumped its contents un-caringly on the floor. Turning it over, she used it as a step stool. Even then, she could barely reach the suitcase handle. Rising on her toes, she was able to just grasp it.

As she pulled it forward, the crate tilted and over balanced. Kali cried out as she fell backwards. She grabbed wildly at the hanging clothes as she fell. Her scream rent the air as her weight bought the metal shelf down upon her as she landed and laid there, eyes closed.

Suwako was just turning away from the window when she heard the scream. Instinct led her to the back of the house. Once there she found a partially opened window but it was too high for her to reach.

Looking about, she spied the patio door. Swiftly she moved to it. She jiggled the lock as hard as she could until the flimsy latch lost the battle of wills.

Entering, she hurried from room to room until she made her way upstairs. Entering the bedroom, she took in the upheaval of the room, clothes thrown everywhere as though a whirlwind had inhabited the premises.

A cry bought her attention to the closet. Moving forward, she caught her breath. Quickly she uncovered the woman, her expression tempered with fear as she took in the white face. As she lifted the metal shelf with the clothes still attached, her foot slipped. Glancing down, she noticed the wetness. Looking closer, she saw it was a mixture of water... and blood.

Kali turned her head slowly to look at Suwako. "What?"

"I say he looks like his father."

Kali looked down at the infant cradled in her arms. "He's mine Suwako."

"And his father's." She insisted. "He is his fathers seed."

Kali tightened her arm protectively, causing the bundle to cry out softly. "He is my son Suwako, mine alone." Kali insisted. Suwako remained silent. "Is that understood Suwako?" She turned from the intensity of the womans stare.

"Nicholi."

"Nicholas." Kali insisted.

"That is good."

Kali glanced up. There was no spite on the other womans face as she studied the child. Kali relaxed her grip.

Kali stood facing the window, gently cooing to Nicholas. "One day there will be beautiful flowers and a playland all your own right outside this door so you can run and play in the sunshine."

The doorbell sounded, just as she turned, Suwako moved silently from the room. Kali turned back to the sunlight and began to softly hum a lullaby.

A moment later she stiffened, her expression growing puzzled. Slowly, almost fearfully she turned. She caught her breath sharply as she took in Nicholi framed in the doorway. Wordlessly she stared as he in turn stared at the child in her arms. Kali pressed him against her breast.

As though in a trance, Nicholi moved towards her. Like one trapped and seeking a way of escape, she looked, her eyes pleading to Suwako who had silently re-entered the room.

Wordlessly the woman crossed the room and gently removed the child from Kali's arms. This done, she carried him from the room. Seeking something to fill her now empty arms, Kali wrapped them about herself.

Nicholi turned from watching Suwako and his son's departure to once again watch her. She shifted uncomfortably. For long moments there was a heavy silence not penetrated by even their breathing. Finally, she turned away, staring blindly out the window. A hand crept up to cover her racing heart, it moved up and down with the force of its beating.

"Why did you keep this from me?" Nicholi spoke into the silence.

"He's my son."

"As though you alone participated in his conception."

"It doesn't matter, I ask nothing of you." She closed her eyes tightly against the tears which threatened, willing herself to show no emotion for surely he would go away.

"You would deny me my child?" She sighed, why was it he never did what she desired? "You owe me at least an answer."

"I owe you nothing and I ask you for nothing."

"And I am to just forget about the child who carries my blood in his veins?"

She could feel his breath against her neck though she had not been aware of any movement on his part. "You have your life, your work, your traditions. Let it be enough and leave us alone to find ours, that's all I'll ever ask of you."

The silence which followed her request sat heavily in the room. She could feel his body straining towards her as her own strained towards him yet neither moved. A delicate cough from the doorway broke the battle as both turned to see Suwako with her suitcase.

"I shall leave now." She spoke softly. Kali moved to stand before her. The two women regarded each other as silent communication wrapped together.

"I don't love you." Kali whispered.

"I know you do." For the first time Suwako smiled. Kali blinked but stood silently as Suwako lifted her case, turned and walked away, never once looking at Nicholi.

"Would you please go?" She spoke without turning.

Nicholi moved to her side. "We will talk."

"But not now." She bowed her head. A moment later she looked up and he was gone.

"I would like for you to view a house with me." Nicholi stood gazing out the window.

Kali raised her head, lowering the papers she had been studying. "Why?"

Nicholi shrugged. "I will be getting married again and I must have a house." Kali's breath caught sharply. Nicholi turned to watch her. "As a friend I ask you to view a possible home with me, that I may have a woman's opinion."

Kali's body began to tremble in outrage. "For the sake of our son I vowed to maintain a civil relationship, but it does not entail assisting you in finding a home for you and the woman you're about to bring into his life."

For a time he only stared, and that was enough. Stubbornly she returned to her papers though her contained tears prevented her from seeing a thing. When she heard the front door close signaling Nicholi's departure, she placed her head on the desk and wept.

Suwako's unexpected return two weeks later was greeted in the same manner as was her departure, Kali stared silently as she was pushed gently to the side allowing the slight woman entry to the house.

Two days later Kali's resistance was low enough for Suwako to override her protests as the slight woman pushed her out the door along with a grocery list, ordering her not to return until her paleness had been replaced with color.

As the door was closed in her face, Kali sighed and looked at the sheet of paper in her hand and caught her breath.

Kali stared up at the house as silent tears fell. "Surely not." she whispered. "Not this, not now." As in a trance she walked to the front door and ran her finger tips lightly over the ornate stained glass panels. A sob escaped her lips.

Nicholi had always been one to keep his word and indeed he had fulfilled his vow.

Kali entered the room self-consciously pulling at the short skirt. Nicholi glanced up from where he sat talking on the phone and froze.

"It's a bit shorter than I'm use to."

"Any how I'll speak to you later." Nicholi quickly replaced the receiver.

"I didn't interrupt did I?"

"Of course you did."

"I'm sorry."

"Don't be, I warned you that if you spoke my sister's name she would call."

Kali's brow rose. "Are you saying that was your sister?"

"It was." Laughter bubbled from her lips. "Trust me, it is not humorous." he responded drily.

"Did you tell her some strange woman was wearing her clothes?"

As his gaze studied her, she felt a blush rise up her neck and cover her face. "I see no strange woman here." he spoke softly.

She cleared her throat nervously. "I-I need to go home and get some shoes." She glanced at the flat shoes on her feet. Nicholi's gaze followed her own.

"I don't think that would be such a good idea." She looked up in puzzlement. "Legs that long should be licensed as it is." The blush rose again. "Maybe I should chance being late and go home and change."

Nicholi rose slowly and moved to stand before her. "I'll make a deal with you..." she swallowed as she stared up at him. "You keep that outfit on and one day I'll build you the house of your dreams."

Shyly she dropped her eyes. "You like it that much?"

He raised her chin with a gentle hand. "I like it that much." His lips lowered.

Kali stood in the rain staring at the house, not quite knowing how she had gotten off the porch. A sob caught in her throat and she closed her eyes. She began to tremble as a jacket was lightly placed about her shoulders. She opened her eyes and moved forward in silence, guided by the hand at her back.

Kali sat on the sofa with her legs curled under, both hands hugging a large mug of coco. In silence Nicholi watched. He took in how his shirt hung partially off her shoulder, leaving her neck vulnerable. His eyes caressed the little pulse beating there. He did not know what had caused her to come to the house but he was thankful she had.

He watched as her lids began to flutter. When she placed the mug on the coffee-table and leaned back against the sofa, he watched. When her lashes laid still on her cheeks, he smiled.

Kali came awake slowly, she stretched out against the warm hard body beside her. A soft purr escaped her lips as she snuggled up against it and returned to the arms of slumber.

Hours later, she awoke to a bed empty but for herself and a dented pillow. Quickly she rose and dressed. As she opened the bedroom door, she looked into the eyes of Suwako. "The little one is asleep, come." The younger woman took her by the hand and lead her away.

"I must go now."

"Why?" Kali questioned.

"I too have discovered what is love."

Kali sighed, "Tell me what it is?"

"It is when you think of someone else's pain instead of feeling your own." She smiled tenderly.

Kali blinked back her tears. "I won't say goodbye."

"No, you've said it too many times already." Suwako opened her arms and Kali flew in.

Nicholi rubbed the back of his neck tiredly. with everything within him he had tried. Now he stood before the glass wall looking at nothing, shoulders slumped in defeat. He closed his eyes and a single tear escaped.

He stiffened as he felt arms wrap around him. He held his breath. He opened his eyes and swallowed the lump in his throat as he felt Kali's lay her head against his back. The pain in his chest reminded him to breathe only for it to be halted yet again as she placed her palms flat against his chest.

The strength of his heart beat had her hands rising and falling with each beat. "May I come home?" Her soft voice whispered through his blood.

For a moment he froze then removed her hands from his chest. As he turned to face her he kept hold of her left wrist. Kali stared up with her heart in her eyes.

With his free hand, Nicholi reached into his pants pocket and without breaking eye contact, he placed her wedding ring on her finger.

As tears began to fall, Kali reached up and wiped them away, her hand a gentle caress against his face. "You've always been home." His voice was husky from the tears. He drew her into his arms. "My hearts always been at home with you." The silence wrapped warm around them as they held each other.

Got It Maid

An arm emerges from the covers, testing the air. Quickly, it strikes out to silence the distress signal emitting from the alarm clock at the bedside. Slowly, Bettina sticks her head out from under the covers like a groundhog after the winter has passed. Staring at the ceiling, a smile slowly breaks forward. Her plainness disappears, eclipsed momentarily by a radiance. She recalls what day it is.

Less than an hour later she is on her way. Laughter bubbles from her lips causing strangers to stare. Many wonder about the lover the young woman is off to greet. Many more find themselves smiling at her love drenched features, for surely it can only be love which makes one so very plain, so very...beauteous.

Once in the elevator, Bettina hums to herself. As the doors open her smile broadens as she views her love. Slowly she approaches, with gentle hands she caresses the form before her. For an instance she closes her eyes. Upon hearing the elevator open behind her, she quickly seats herself. With one lingering pat she whispers, "Hello my love." Her love replies with a flash of lights. Bettina's shift has begun, Kato and Company is now open for business. Bettina Clemans, the daytime switchboard operator is in place. The calls begin.

"You have got to be kidding Charis."

"India..."

"You have her in love with a switchboard for goodness sake!"

"It's something different.

"Maybe too different."

"People get tired of the same old thing."

"Same old thing? Um Charis, how long since your last date?"

"What has that to do with my writing?" Charis Pearces shifted uncomfortably in her seat as she avoided the eyes of her agent and friend.

"More than you know honey."

"So what are you saying agent of mine? What do you want?"

"I'd like to make a few...suggestions if I may."

"Can I stop you?" She sighed heavily.

"No...look, you're a good writer..."

"Only good?" One delicately arched brow rose to maximum capacity.

"Good. You've had three fairly successful books. They could have been better."

"Tell me how oh great one."

"I'm not kidding Charis."

Charis became serious as she looked at her friend. "Okay India, sorry."

"More depth."

"More what?"

"More depth, as in emotions. All of your main characters are becoming you or vice versa. I'm not certain which is worst."

"India..."

"When was the last time you went out?"

"Last week, we had lunch."

India looked up to the ceiling as though in silent prayer. "I mean a date, as in with a man...for pleasure purposes."

She stared at the young woman without blinking. "Easy...it was...ah."

"That long huh?"

Charis looked sheepish, she shrugged. "So what's wrong with the book?"

"Not since you and Stan broke up." India refused to be side tracked.

"So?"

"Sweetheart, that was five years ago. I mean, don't you ever get the urge?"

"Urge?" Charis was puzzled.

"To merge."

"Humph, it quickly passes."

India sat back in her chair, this time it was her eyebrow which rose. "You don't say?"

"You don't like the book."

"It would probably sell but it's not your best work."

"So you're saying."

"How's that story going, you know the mistaken identity. The one with the maid?"

"It's going no where. I'm working on something else."

"Can something else for awhile, I have an idea. My mom owns a domestic service. She started it up after the divorce. It's doing great business."

"So..." Charis was suspicious.

"Why don't you go undercover for awhile?"

"Under whose cover?"

"You know, like research. See how your character really lives."

"India Hansford, I don't have to be a maid just to write about one!"

"It will give you insight, more depth. Make her real."

"India..."

"Think about it, it'll only be a little while. Your character will be three dimensional and what can go wrong? Besides, mom's in a tough spot right now. She could use a little help."

"Then why don't you help?"

"You want to take over my job?" India smiled smugly as she leaned forward anticipating Charis' answer.

"And deal with dragon lady Helen Tyler, no way. I'll take being a maid over that task any day."

"You are so very kind."

Charis smiled contently, "I know, it's one of my virtues, numerous though they are."

As Charis sat before the desk her face held every emotion but agreement. The elegantly dressed woman standing before the window turned away from her to mask a smile. "It doesn't take much. The man already has a housekeeper and a cleaning staff."

"So why does he need another maid?"

Now composed, Lily Hansford, a beautiful woman of fifty-four, turned to face the young woman who sat uneasily at the edge of her seat. "Charis, he doesn't need another maid. He needs someone to watch over the kids."

Charis twitched arrogantly, "Well, I don't do kids."

"It wouldn't be for long."

"You mean you want me to be like...a nanny?"

"You could say that."

"Couldn't you like try Brooklyn?" she joked.

Lily laughed in delight. "That only happens on television. Come on Charis, what's there to be afraid of?"

"Remember what happened the last time I did what India asked?"

Lilys' laughter ended abruptly. "Indie swore she didn't know it was a topless bar."

Charis' eyebrow shot up, her expression showing she was not entirely convinced of her friends innocence.

For the fifteenth-million time, Charis pushed the thick framed black glasses back in place. Her hair was pulled back so tightly she felt as though she was the victim of a discount facelift. "Oh India I owe you and be certain I fully intend to pay you back with high interest." she muttered to herself.

"Pardon?"

She turned and focused upon the two children facing her. Quickly, she replayed her information file silently to herself. The young girl, age twelve, was LaPennie. She was a willowy looking child. Hair and eyes a rather limp brown. The boy, age nine, was Martin. He was a sturdy child. Hair golden yet dull like the sun peeking from behind a cloud, eyes like his sister with the exception of the added spark of innocence not yet extinguished by life which was sadly missing from the eldest child. It made her appear much older than her natural years.

Charis shook herself mentally, reminding herself she was not there to get involved. "So what's your schedule?" She asked.

With nary an emotion, the two recited their daily itinerary while Charis suppressed a yawn.

"Indie you wouldn't believe this place, it's like a funeral home and you can't tell the stiffs from the living."

"It can't be that bad."

Charis tightened her grip on the receiver. "Get me out of this one and I'll forgive you for everything you're ever done plus give you a two week grace period."

"That bad huh?" There was silence. "That bad." She sighed.

"Well India, when are you springing me?" There was silence. Charis' voice held a note of desperation, "India, come on now, don't do this. These kids are really miniature adults, they don't need me. They're so perfect and boring it makes me feel I'm the one in need of a nanny."

India finally spoke. "Mom needs you to stay on, at least for a little while longer. She hasn't been able to come up with anyone else just yet."

"Are you certain she's looking?" There was silence. "When I get out of this one I'm coming collecting." Charis replaced the receiver abruptly. She knew eventually she would forgive her best friend but for the moment she savored her anger. She squared her shoulders and a militant glint entered her eyes. "I declare war on this place." She glanced around the dark and gloomy library.

Her steps determined, she approached a bookshelf. With a wicked smile, she rearranged the books and stood back, taking in her handy work. The shelves, once neatly arranged by size were now mixed, the once smooth lines broken. Charis gave a short laugh. "I claim this land in the name of life!" Eyes shining, she marched from the room.

"But our clothes aren't too small." Martin insisted.

Charis looked back in amazement. "Is that the only time you get new clothes?"

"Not at all, there's always Christmas." LaPennie supplied in her deadpan voice.

"Really, how very...exciting."

"Not really." LaPennie commented.

Charis stopped abruptly, almost getting smacked by the revolving door in the process. "What is this, what is this I hear? Could it be a slight sense of humor, a wise crack even?"

"Not likely." LaPennie droned before entering the door, a brief smile flirting about her lips. The dawning of a twinkle entered her eye. Martin followed her into the store.

Charis stood on the sidewalk shaking her head. "Well, I'll be a..." She smiled as she saw the kids gesturing through the glass for her to enter.

"Now I will be gone approximately three weeks. Nothing should come up which would need my immediate attention."

"It wouldn't dare." Charis muttered.

"Excuse me" Mason Chattsworth questioned. Charis gave him a look of total innocence. "Anyhow, Annia and Alvin know the routine should some circumstance arrive in which you must contact me."

"How nice"

He turned to face her. "What did you say?"

"I hope it's a nice trip.' She lied.

"It's a business trip." He stated as though she should have known better.

"Of course."

He turned away, dismissing her from his presence. Charis shrugged then moved to leave the room. As she stepped to the doorway, the children appeared as though summoned. They avoided each others eyes.

A few moments later found them gathered in the hallway waving as Mason climbed into a big black bug-looking car. As the vehicle drew away Charis closed the front door. Slowly she turned to the statue-like children. For a second no one moved, then slowly a smile appeared on their faces. "Lets party." Charis stated simply.

"Kids, I'll never understand them."

"Trouble in play land Ma'am?" Charis stared at Alvin the butler as he placed a saucer with fruit before her.

Her ready sarcasm died as she looked up at him. "One day we're having a ball, the next we're back to square one."

"It's that time of the year Ma'am."

Her puzzlement showed. "That time of the year?" Alvin didn't respond. "Come on, give."

"Birthday Ma'am. It's her thirteenth."

"What do they normally do for their birthdays?"

"Sulk." Annia the housekeeper announced as she entered. "Poor dears, their papa is usually so busy he forgets till days later."

"Once he was a month late, thus the antique hobby horse." Alvin supplied.

"Which is too expensive for them to ride." Annia added in disgust. "Can't you do something? You're young. Because of you, for the first time laughter flows through these halls."

"Shocking isn't it?" Alvin droned.

Annia elbowed him. "But very welcome."

"So what are you going to do?" This from Alvin.

"Me?" Charis watched his eyebrow rise. "We could..." She looked for some help but the older couple only stared. "I hate kids." She looked away. Annia and Alvin turned away.

"This is going to be fun." Alvin nodded to Annia, his tone deadpan.

"Come on Annia, you can do it!" The children urged. The sound of laughter radiated through the halls.

"Alvin did it." Martin stated.

"Indeed." She agreed as she stared down from the top step of the spiral staircase. "But Alvin does not have as many body parts to watch out for."

"Only the family jewels." The hero in question stated with a straight face.

"What, you mean they haven't been pawned?" Annia shot in response as she secured her hiked skirt in the waistband of her belt. "Well, anything that old man can do I can surely do." She grunted as she threw a leg over the banister. Saying a silent prayer she closed her eyes and shoved off.

The children laughed as she slid down the banister, looking much like she was riding a wild horse. As she reached the bottom, the laughter ended abruptly. Annia opened her eyes.

Alvin quickly moved forward to help her dismount and smooth her uniform in its rigid place as Mason who stood in the front doorway looked on in grim disapproval.

"Is this what I am to expect every time I leave my home?"

He took in the group. "Total chaos? Alvin and Annia, I expected more of you. As for you Ms. Pearces, you may well be use to hooligans as your charge but I expect my children to spend their time in more worthwhile pursuits. I expect them to act like adults."

"But they're not adults, they're children. And as children they should be allowed to have fun" Charis defended hotly.

"They can have fun later when they've achieved something, made something of themselves."

"Like you I guess."

"Explain yourself." He demanded.

"With pleasure, everyone can see how much fun you're having. You expect them to look forward to that?"

Masons' face became stone. "Since you do not seem to be capable of abiding by my rules, I deem it necessary for you to leave immediately Ms. Pearces."

There was a collective gasp from the group. Charis turned and silently made her way up the stairs. "Anyone else who has trouble with my rules may join her." Mason stated coldly. The remainder of the hall occupants drifted silently away.

As Charis came down the stairs with her suitcases, Alvin appeared as though summoned. Silently he met her, taking the cases, he walked beside her down the remainder of the stairway and to the door. Once there, he sat the cases down and turned.

"You did what was right. At least now they will have some fond memories."

Charis swallowed and nodded. "Guess you better hide the trampoline." She smiled weakly. There was a blow of a horn and she opened the door. Alvin retrieved the cases and walked out with her to the taxi.

After the driver had placed her bags in the trunk, she turned to Alvin. "Take care ma'am." He stated gruffly, she could only shake her head. She glanced back at the house. In an upper window, she watched as LaPennie pulled back from sight. Charis ducked her head and climbed into the taxi. Alvin closed the door after briefly touching the back of her hand which rested on the lowered window. The taxi pulled away as he took a deep breath and walked back up the stairs to the house.

"It's for the best, you wanted out and anyhow you know how you hate children." India stared at Charis downcast face.

"People say a lot of things, besides, the kids weren't so bad once you got to know them."

"Ah, what a confession from the unreachable Ms. Charis Pearces." India turned away from the tears in her friends' eyes.

"You have what you insisted upon."

"Excuse me?" Mason glanced from the stack of papers before him, his hand freezing on its trip to the briefcase to his left. "What did you say Annia?" He gave an absent-minded smile.

"Your children are once more locked in their rooms acting like the adults they aren't, stripped of anything which could mistakenly be considered emotions."

His smile shattered. "Now see here Annia. I have looked upon you as family..."

Annia was on a roll which even a brick wall could not have halted. "You don't even treat your own family as a family. I truly don't understand why you and the Misses separated, being that you became her. You should get along fine now." She turned to leave.

"Wait a minute, you can't leave after dropping that! I'm nothing like my ex-wife!"

"You're quite right sir." She turned to look over her shoulder. "She did have enough decency to leave the children, you stay and deny their right to live their lives anyway other than how you've mapped them out."

Mason was dumbfound "You've never spoken in this manner Annia."

"Much to my everlasting shame I'm sure." She left the room.

Mason sat back, his paperwork forgotten, his face a picture of surprised concentration.

Mason stood for a moment and observed his eldest as she sat on the window seat staring out at the falling rain. LaPennie was the picture of dejection and for the first time he noted it and it tore at his heart. "What's the matter princess?" He spoke softly.

For a moment she didn't respond, then slowly turned her sad face to stare at him. "Our first mommy left us but you ran this one away. You know what? It didn't hurt this bad the first time." Ignoring his shocked expression she rose and moved beyond him and out the door.

"Yes Mrs. Hogarth, I will be contacting you with a decision." Mason ushered the woman out of the office. "Fifty-two my big-toe, I bet you're not a week under one hundred." He whispered under his breath.

"Now I need to know in a few days at most. Can't just waste time waiting around for you can I?"

"I just know you can't." His sarcasm was wasted on the applicant. He smiled politely.

He was about to call the next applicant seated when he happened to glance through the door into the hallway. "Ladies I thank you for your time but we have reached a decision, thank you."

The three remaining applicants looked first at each other, then Mason. Silently they rose and headed for the door adjusting scarves, coats and gloves with open disapproval and disappoint- ment. As the women filed out, Charis stepped forward to join the procession.

"Ms Pearces, if you would step into my office please."

The women turned to look at Charis then abruptly continued out. Charis cautiously made her way to Mason. They examined each other for a moment.

Without a word she turned and made her way back to the hallway. She picked up her suitcases and after a glance at the still silent Mason, turned and headed towards the stairs.

Alvin appeared and relieved her of the bags and led the way up. Mason watched the pair from the doorway of the office; his arms folded and a faint smile upon his lips.

After he had turned and reentered the room, Annia and the children exchanged silent high fives and drew back into the library.

"Earth to Charis, earth to Charis, come in please."

Charis refocused on India's face, "What were you saying?"

"Which part did I lose you on?"

"Could you start at the beginning?" She smiled sheepishly.

"Guess it's fortunate for me you're a better writer than listener."

"Sorry."

"Don't be. The book's coming along great."

"So glad Madam taskmaster is please."

"If I weren't you wouldn't be at the plush Terra Royale enjoying yourself." India's expression was skeptic. "At least enjoying yourself was the purpose of this get away."

"It's beautiful."

"Yes, the snow is lovely."

"Truly."

"There is no snow Charis."

Charis turned to look out the wall length glass windows at her side. "Oh."

"Want to tell India about it?"

"He did it again."

"Fired you?"

"Left the children. He's never there for them. It's one business trip after the other with the children left on the sidelines. I thought after I came back that he would change, at least try to. The only difference now is he doesn't yell when he comes back."

"What is it you want or expect him to do?"

Charis sighed. "Every once and awhile put the children first. Cancel one meeting to be with them."

"Where's he now?"

"Yet another trip, he was suppose to be back yesterday but he extended it. I hated to leave LaPennie and Martin alone."

"I thought Alvin and Annia were there."

"They are but..."

"Careful Charis." India warned. "You're falling for those kids and that's more fatal then falling for a man."

Charis stared at her dearest friend. "Just remember you sent me on this job." Charis smiled. It was not returned.

Charis scanned the crowded room for the third time. "India where are you?" The movement of the bar swirled around her. She moved to allow the group of men entering to pass. She was blind to their admiring glances as she scanned the room yet again. Sighing, she moved from her station by the archway and made her way across the room to the bar.

Seating herself upon a vacant stool she turned sideways so to keep an eye on the door. "What'll it be gorgeous?" The bartender asked.

Charis turned absently towards him. "Cherry Cola if you have it."

"For you I'd send someone out to get it if I didn't."

Charis gave him a slight smile. "You mean you wouldn't go yourself?"

"And leave you alone? I think not. I'm polite but not stupid."

They both laughed. As he prepared her drink she turned once again towards the door. As she did, her elbow came in contact with a solid body. "Pardon me." She threw over her shoulder then froze. There on her left stood Mason.

"If you have to be decked, it pays to have a beautiful woman do it, wouldn't you say Eddi?" Mason shared a smile with the bartender.

Charis voice came out encased in frost. "Did you come up with that all by yourself?"

Masons' expression became puzzled, she turned away. Eddi shrugged as Mason looked to him in question. He sat down and tried again. "May I buy you a drink?"

"Even if they weren't free I wouldn't let you buy me anything." Charis spat before taking the drink the bartender sat before her, standing and walking away.

Mason looked to Eddi again. "Was it something I said?"

"Whatever it was I wouldn't say it again." The bartender warned. Mason looked after Charis' retreating figure.

"Ogres are looking better and better now days." India joked as she watched Mason across the span of the room.

"If that's your type." Charis commented dryly "Friend, that type is always on the top of my list, if not I'll make room for him." She looked at her friend in disbelief. "Don't try to tell me he's not your type."

"He's fine if you like the noncaring type."

India stared at the object of their conversation. "Looks like he could care a lot."

Charis gave a unladylike snort. "Next topic of conversation please."

India faced her reluctantly. "Pity, he looks good for at least a five course...plus dessert." Charis stared at her in disbelief, India only shrugged.

Charis' stride was angry as she made her way down the hall. "I could just kill and pull the time. Temporary insanity is what they'd charge. I could get a rest and write a book at the same time. Heck, selling movie rights would be a snap." She fumed.

"Is that so?"

She came to an abrupt halt and swung around, almost over-balancing in the process. Mason stood not three feet away. Without a verbal response, she turned and continued down the corridor. He followed.

Charis halted before her room. Fumbling, she drew her key from her clutch which was more cute then practical. As she moved to insert the key in the keyhole, Mason covered it.

"What could I possibly have done to make you so angry with me?

"Move your hand." She demanded.

"Do you just make a habit to pick a stranger to be the object of your disgust?"

She moved to physically remove his hand but stopped just short of touching him. A rush of expelled breath rushed past her ear as he noted the action. "What have I done to make you hate me?"

In a whirl she turned, almost snarling. "Not a thing. Lets just say for the record that when I turned thirteen my father forgot my birthday because he was too busy with the business and I've hated men like you every since." She turned back and shoved his hand away from the door knob, taking him by surprise.

By the time he had recovered, she had opened the door and was entering. Just as she went to slam it he moved, blocking it with his body. "Get out of my..."

"May as well be condemned for the cow rather than just the milk." He grabbed her shoulders and yanked hard, causing her to stumble. Before she could recover he seized her lips in a hard kiss.

Just as quickly he released her and walked away, never noticing the tears in her eyes.

Charis stiffened in her seat, even without a word being spoken she knew Mason stood behind her. "I only wanted to apologize for last night." Seated across from her, India's brow flew up. Charis felt her face turning red. "Will you at least look at me if I promise to drop off the face of the earth?" he continued.

"Please don't do that." India injected with a saucy smile. Charis groaned softly for she knew what was about to happen and couldn't find the strength to prevent it. "Please join us."

She felt his gaze on her but sat frozen, her eyes pleading with India who chose to ignore her. "I insist. I'm certain you're the most interesting man I've never known... and I've never known quite a few." She smiled wickedly, "Not as many as Charis here but still quite a few." Charis closed her eyes and turned away.

How was it possible? Charis thought as she stared at Mason. How could she have possibly enjoyed the past two hours she had spent with a man she detested? And why did she feel such jealousy every time he turned that lethal smile on India?

She shook her heads as though it would clear it. "You don't agree?" Mason asked her, his smile at half mast yet still brilliant.

Charis felt the color flood her cheeks. "I'm sorry, my thoughts wandered for a moment."

"I know business is boring. I must apologize..."

India cut him off. "Oh not at all, it's refreshing to see a man who can gush... about business and family."

Mason smiled with a boyish charm and Charis thought maybe it was a good thing that he didn't smile often. "I know the world of Corporate Finance and children can never be as exciting as writing."

This time Charis interrupted. "I loved hearing about your children. They sound wonderful. A lot better than sitting behind a big desk locked over a keyboard." She lowered her head shyly at the intensity of his regard.

"They are, I only wish I could spend more time with them, though in all honesty I only recently came to realize just how little time we do share."

India rose to his defense. "A man in your position..."

"A man in my position shouldn't have allowed himself to become blinded about what's important and lasting." They sat in silence for a moment. "Ladies... I was planning to ask you to join me for dinner tonight but I believe I'll be returning home today."

Charis stared in shock. "But there's three more days of meetings!"

Mason stared. "I will be returning home. I have a number of loose ends to tie up. Number one is begging the forgiveness of a certain young lady whose birthday I regrettably missed."

"I didn't mean..." Charis started but his hand on hers placed her at a loss for words.

"You did and rightly so." He squeezed the hand he covered. "And it's about time."

"I guess we'll have to get back to work with no distractions now." India injected, causing Charis to jerk her hand from beneath Mason's. For an instant he frowned then his brows smoothed out again.

"I hope to see you ladies again real soon." He spoke as he rose.

"Count on it." India's smile widened. Charis dropped her head and swallowed.

"I don't care, I'm not going." Charis fumed as she marched about India's office.

India looked on with a smile of amusement playing hide-and-seek with her lips. "The invitation's for both of us."

Charis turned, stopping short of snarling... barely. "I don't care." Her words were clipped. "I know what he's up to and I will not be a witness to it."

India turned her escaped chuckle into a cough. "How do you know it's an engagement party?"

Charis regarded her confidant as though she had just sprouted a second head. "Did you hear me when I told you about all the arrangements I've had to make this past week?" India's mouth opened but she wasn't given the time to speak. "Besides, I told you he took the kids in his study and told them he was remarrying. Now this party."

"Even if it is, isn't this what you wanted?"

"What I wanted?!" Charis exclaimed.

"You said they needed a mother not a nanny. It's a shot at a normal life." India shrugged.

"Not with the type women he has about. they'll never love those kids..." She stopped abruptly.

India regarded her sadly, all humor gone. "The way you do?" She rose and moved around her desk. "It's a fine mess you've gotten yourself into friend." She took the now sobbing woman in her arms.

Mason smiled foolishly at his children who stood like toy soldiers before him. "Isn't it great?" LaPennie and Martin exchanged glances. "You'll get to meet your future mom in a little while. I know you're going to love her."

For a moment all was silent. LaPennie took a deep breath but it was Martin who spoke. "I doubt it." He threw out before racing from the room, taking Mason by surprise. Her eyes downcast, LaPennie followed leaving a speechless Mason behind.

Before he could pull himself together the doorway was filled with the tightly sheathed body of a bleach blonde. Her skin fitting silver gown clung to all parts, real and otherwise. Godiva, the ex-wife of his business partner slid up to him. "Come on darling, lets get back to the party. You said you had a very important announcement to make tonight. I'm just tingling all over in anticipation."

"The kids..."

"Will be kids, come on, the guests are waiting." She attached herself to his side and pulled him from the study, her smile as false as her body.

Mason stared for what felt like the hundredth time towards the doorway and sighed. Godiva's face hardened then quickly relaxed. "Looking for someone?"

"A friend." She frowned. "I expected..." His voice trailed off as he absently untangled himself from her grasp. She followed the direction of his gaze. Her features hardened again as she watched India and Charis enter. Mason moved in their direction as though hypnotized.

Charis could feel his stare from across the room. Her skin became hot and her breathing strangely disturbed. "Take it easy girl." India whispered gently just before Mason reached them.

"I'm glad the two of you made it, I was beginning to... wonder." He smiled at India then fixed his gaze on Charis. She avoided looking at him.

"Nice little turn-out." India watched.

"Yes. It's a special night and I wanted to share it with friends." He willed Charis to look at him but she refused. His brow wrinkled.

"It's nice to be considered friends after so brief an acquaintance." India tossed into the void.

"A person can go from acquaintance to friend in just the time it takes to look at them and truly see them." He whispered.

Charis turned startled eyes to him and was lost. "Will you dance with me?" She watched his lips and felt herself being drawn in.

"There you are." As though they had been suddenly drenched in ice water the trio turned as one. Godiva stood before them. "Mr. Coctrerey says he absolutely must speak to you about that merger, it's an emergency."

Mason turned to Charis. "I have to speak to him, it's a very delicate situation right now." She turned away. Mason reached out and gently touched her arm. "Promise you'll dance with ma as soon as I return." His voice was low and intimate. "Please. It would mean so much." His hand caressed her arm. "Please." She nodded without looking at him.

No one noticed the fury in Godiva's eyes which was quickly hidden when Mason turned to her... no one except India who looked on thoughtfully.

Charis closed her eyes and took a deep breath. Slowly, she opened her eyes and turned. Godiva stood blocking the bathroom door. "It was so... nice of you and your... friend to come to Mason's...party."

"We were invited, we came."

Godiva came further into the room. Standing before the mirror, she arrogantly touched her starched hair. 'Yes, well Mason is so happy things have finally been worked through, he wants to share that happiness with everyone."

Charis moved closer to the door. We're just glad my ex-husband finally, how should we say... saw the light. He and Mason aren't partners anymore so there's really no interference now."

"How nice." Charis' voice was dry yet her face was expressionless.

"Yes, thus the engage... I mean the party."

Charis took her time in looking over the woman before her, when she spoke her voice was cold. "I wonder how the children feel about all this."

Godiva flushed with anger. Her voice was heated. "It doesn't matter. They'll be gone after the wedding." She turned in anger towards the mirror. Without another word, Charis turned away in disgust and left the room.

"Perhaps you should take a little stroll to cool off."

"What makes you think I'm hot?" Charis avoided India's amused gaze.

"I don't know. Perhaps the steam coming from your ears."

"Are you really my friend?" Charis turned to her.

India's face softened and she gently touched her arm. "Always. Now take a walk until you can get your mask straight." Charis turned away, India touched her shoulder. "Go by way of the playroom." Charis nodded in gratitude and moved off.

Charis stood silently watching the two dejected children from the doorway. LaPennie and Martin sat on the edge of the trampoline with heads bowed. Martin was leaned into his sisters' side. Charis' heart squeezed at the sight, causing her to put aside her own hurt.

With gentle yet firm determination she entered. "Is this a private party or can anyone join?"

The children jerked up in surprise. "There's no party here ma'am." LaPennie informed her in a tight voice. "My brother and I were just..." Her words ceased abruptly as she stared at the beautiful woman. Her mouth opened but no sound came forth.

Her eyes filled with tears. "CeCe?" She jumped from the trampoline and flew across the room, Martin close behind her. Charis opened her arms and received them both mindless of her black velvet evening gown. Both children cried as they clung to her.

A short time later all three sat on the trampoline's edge, the children's tears a mere sniffling. "Does this mean you're happy to see me or not?"

The kids giggled. "You sure clean up pretty good." Martin stated innocently.

"So what exactly are you saying I look like at other times?" Both children smiled sheepishly. "I see." They giggled again.

"Have daddy seen you yet?" LaPennie asked hopefully. "Yes."

"Do he know it's you?" Martin followed.

Charis didn't reply. "It's okay, he doesn't know you like we do." For a moment there was silence. "I wish he did." LaPennie ended.

"So why aren't you guys at the party?"

A mutinous look settled on both their faces. "Queen Godiva didn't think it appropriate." LaPennie spat.

"She has that much pull huh?"

"It's not like she ain't been sniffing around Daddy long enough."

Martin shook his head at his sister's comment. "Every since Mom left. Even when her husband was around."

"Mason didn't say anything?"

LaPennie laughed without humor. "You know daddy, he never see what's right in front of him..."

"If it's not business." Martin completed for her. Both of them regarded Charis.

"Know what we mean?" LaPennie asked pointedly.

This time it was Charis' turn to flush. "So how do you two feel?"

"She doesn't like us."

"Doesn't care for us at all." Martin completed his sister's comment again.

"Let us know it every chance she gets."

Martin nodded, "Yeah, told us if she have her way we're out of here."

Charis' eyes began to blaze but instantly lost their fire as LaPennie snuggled into her side. "She's not like you." She whispered.

Charis swallowed. "Maybe she just needs a little time to get to know you like I did." Both kids drew away to look at her. "Hey, I wasn't too hot on the idea at first but you grew on me... kind of like fungus." They laughed as she had intended but the mood quickly grew somber again.

"But she's not you." LaPennie whispered.

Martin shook his head in agreement. "She's not you." The trio sat silently.

Suddenly Charis kicked off her pumps and began hitching up her gown. She maneuvered until she was standing on the surface of the trampoline. "Lets put some party in this party." The kids immediately joined her and their laughter rang out.

They paused only for a moment as the door opened and India walked inn. Charis called out for her to join them but she laughingly declined with, "Me on that is a sight you really don't want to see. trust me on this one."

They were all laughing when Godiva sauntered in. For a moment no one was aware of her presence until her shrill voice cut into their merriment. All action froze in surprise.

"I don't know how Mason forces himself to keep you two around with you constantly disgracing him!"

LaPennie and Martin tucked themselves in Charis side and clung. Seeing it, Godiva's voice rose until she was screaming. "You darn brats need discipline and a boarding school in the middle of nowhere is where you're going to get it. I'll see to it you little monsters!"

Wordlessly Charis moved and lowered herself to the floor. The children followed suit.

"Your own mother couldn't stand the sight or sound of you!"

Charis handed them their shoes which they quickly put on all the while keeping their eyes glued to her face alone which incited Godiva all the more. Out of nowhere Annia appeared, Charis nodded and gently pushed the children in her direction. They walked with heads high past the fuming Godiva and out the room.

Charis replaced her own shoes and glided across the floor, India following in silence. With each non-responsive step Charis took, Godiva's rage expanded itself.

All the occupants of the living room swung about in shock at the angry words being screamed. they looked on in disbelief as Godiva trailed a still silent Charis spewing out her venomous words.

All movement ceased as Charis crossed the room and moved towards the sliding doors which led to outside. Godiva followed closely ignoring the guests. India followed wordlessly. "It's junk like you that shouldn't be allowed about decent people. I don't know how you wormed your way in here but I'll be damned if I allow you to stay!"

Charis, still silent, opened the door, Godiva followed. A stunned Mason just entering the room froze. The elderly man he stood with touched his arm in warning but he shook him away, his own face becoming like a storm cloud as he passed along the route the women had taken.

Once outside, Charis turned to face Godiva. When she spoke her voice was soft. "Have you quite finished?"

"Not by a long shot." She barked. "I know all about your little ploy to trap Mason just like that good for nothing nanny tried. And I'll be damned if I'll allow it as long as I've been working on him. You've best stick to your own no-class kind!"

Charis stepped towards her. Godiva's bravo abruptly faded before the flames in her eyes. She stepped back to escape the fire. "Your opinion of me doesn't matter but you will not hurt those children with your vile tongue."

Her words were spoken softly, yet Godiva continued to involuntarily retreat.

Her foot slipped and she caught herself, glancing over her shoulder she found herself at the edge of the pool. In a panic, her eyes flew to Charis. "You wouldn't!" She hissed.

"I would." Charis' tone never changed.

There was a great splash as Godiva hit the water. Mason had just managed to break through the crowd which had followed the pair when Godiva's head broke the waters surface.

"Mason!" She screamed, taking in a mouth full of water. But Mason's eyes were fixed on Charis whose look had turned defiant as she turned to face him.

"I didn't know you were into slumming." She glanced over her shoulder at the floundering Godiva. "You better get a net." She faced him. "There's trash in your pool. The guests began to snicker as she walked away. Mason attempted to follow but was unable to as the people pressed around him to re-enter the house. No one took notice of the still screaming woman in the pool. India stood by the door silently applauding. One of the guests commented. "Don't you just love parties?"

Charis scrambled to reach the manically ringing phone, knocking pages of manuscript everywhere in the process. Upon achieving picking up the phone, she promptly dropped it.

"Darn it all!" She exclaimed as she succeeded in trapping it yet again in the crook of her neck.

"Well, if that's the way you feel about it." Came a muffled response.

"Hello?"

"What are you destroying?"

"It's you."

Greetings and salutations to you too." India laughed.

"Sorry."

"I know but I haven't held it against you all these years so why start now?"

"India..."

"Okay party pooper. How are things going?"

"Busy. I'm almost finished."

"I truly hate to say this but..." She took an exaggerated breath. "You're working too hard."

"Never heard of it."

"Don't record this conversation because I don't want it to haunt me, but you're working too hard friend."

"Do you want the book?"

"Of course, it's your best work, but I would like to have you around after I've gotten my commission. Only because I want to collect more understand."

"I'm a big girl India, honest."

"You've become a workaholic."

"You have to go while the flow is flowing."

"Just don't end up flooding yourself okay?"

"Got to go Indie."

"Charis."

"Talk to you later." Hurriedly, she hung up. "You don't understand, if I keep writing I can't think, if I can't think, I won't hurt, If I don't hurt, I won't..." Tears began to fall.

"Is she alright? She is gonna be all right... isn't she?"

Charis turned her head cautiously on the pillow towards the whisper. LaPennie and Martin stood peeking into the room. Her eyes closed again, the whispers becoming muffled.

"We just wanted to see if she was awake yet.' LaPennie spoke over her shoulder before moving aside.

Charis' eyes snapped open when she felt a hand placed on her forehead. "I tried to tell you that you were working too hard." Before she could think of a response, Mason turned to the kids. "Into the kitchen kids. Mommy will probably be up soon."

Charis' eyes closed, this time intentionally attempting to block out the painful words. "Well honey, do you think you can get up today?" The hand returned to her cheek. Her eyes opened, puzzled. Mason sighed. "Okay, you just rest some more. I'm going to take the kids out so it should be pretty quiet. Annia's still here if you need anything." He bent and gave her a leisurely kiss.

He was smiling when he straightened. "The kids keep asking when they're going to get their mom back. When am I going to get my wife back?" He whispered suggestively as he raised her hand to his lips. A quick smile and he was gone.

Stunned, Charis raised her hand to touch her forehead. Mid-way to its mark, she froze as the sunlight sent sparkles from her finger. Her breath caught as she stared at the wedding ring.

Lightening shot through her body, causing her to spring from the bed in blind panic. She raced to the kitchen.

"Mom's up!" The joyful screams assaulted her. The children rushed to hug her. Charis automatically returned the embraces but was rendered speechless.

"Hey, I thought you'd be laying down a little longer."

"Well, I for one am glad you're up and about Mrs. Chattsworth." Annia spoke from her position by the sink.

Charis' mouth opened but no words came out. Mason came up to her. "Got to keep my promises. The kids and I'll be back in a little bit." He gave her a quick peck and ushered the protesting kids through the door. Annia quietly disappeared through another door, leaving a very confused Charis alone.

She moved to stare out the window above the sink, her bumped the phone on the counter. Coming to herself, she quickly dialed. After only a couple rings, India answered.

"India, thank God!"

"Charis, hey, long time no hear from you. How's the family doing?"

She went weak in the knees and sought out a kitchen chair before her legs gave way.

A half an hour later and she was even more confused. "How can I not remember getting married?" She stared at the rings on her finger as her hand laid in her lap. Tears made her eyes shine almost as bright as the diamonds on her finger.

Charis feigned sleep. The bed moved as Mason shifted on the other side. "Are you all right?" She jerked at the sound of his voice. "Honey?"

She swallowed. "Just thinking." Her voice came out faint.

"You really should take some time to just relax. You work too hard. You're becoming as bad as I was."

"God forbid."

"Ah, the little woman is coming back to life."

She turned to face him, prepared for a battle of words. Looking into his eyes made her ready words flee. "What, nothing to say? And you a well versed writer." He laughed, the sound husky Charis could only stare, her eyes fixed on his mouth.

The laugh ceased abruptly. Her eyes traveled upward. She was unaware of the longing on her face. "I guess I should let you get some rest." She only stared. "We want you back to your old self."

"Sure." She whispered.

"Right." His voice lowered as did his head.

She welcomed the pressure of his chest. How could she have ever forgotten this? She thought. She sighed, feeling like she had come home at last.

The kisses started slow but with each building upon the last, they became longer and deeper. Charis began to caress Mason's back taking extreme pleasure in the feel of the smoothness of his skin and the power of his muscles even in their relaxed state.

A soft moan issued from her lips against his. Abruptly, he drew back. "I... um. You know..." He began to draw back. "I um... feel we're not quite as close as we use to be. You're a little withdrawn. Maybe we should work at rebuilding our relationship. you know, start the courtship all over. We could both use it."

Hurriedly he moved from the bed, his movements comic in his haste. "I think I'll move into the spare bedroom for a little while. Just to give you a little time." He backed from the room, bumping into the chair and almost falling in the process. Charis raised up on her elbows in amazement. The door was closed just short of being slammed...just. "No he didn't.' She whispered in amazement.

On the other side of the door, Mason leaned against it, eyes closed, breathing hard. "No I didn't." He whispered in amazement. Straightening, he walked stiffly down the hallway.

Mason entered the room. Almost immediately he peeked back down the hall at the other bedroom door... and groaned. "Oh yes I did." He moved back into the room and closed the door.

Mason sighed as the hands worked their magic on his back. The pillow wrapped about his head muffled the sound. He smiled as gentle kisses trailed his back. "Oh Charis."

"Yes." came the response.

He smiled again, then froze, his eyes snapping open. In a flurry of movement he turned helter-skelter until he had flipped over onto his back causing himself to be wrapped cocoon like in the covers.

Before he could speak, Charis had mounted the bed and was anchored over him. "Hi." She whispered. He swallowed again, almost choking in the process.

She bent to kiss him. "Can I sleep with you?" She tried to unwrap him but he pulled the cover up as she attempted to pull it down. "The bed is so big... and lonely." She kissed him again.

Teasing, she sung throatily, "Lets make music together, lets make sweet harmony. Lets make music together, just you and me." She kissed him yet again... deeply.

When it broke off he was breathless. "Will you marry me?" He squealed in a rush.

"Again? You're so silly." She smiled seductively. She ran her hand from his cheek to his chest and went to move lower. He seized it.

"Um. I mean for the first time." She bent forward, trapping his hand between her breast and his chest. She nuzzled his neck. "We're not married!" He belted out in panic.

She paused frowning slightly. "What are you playing at?"

Mason swallowed. "You're really going to laugh when you hear this. It's a joke really." Charis drew back a little. "It's really funny when you think about it."

She drew back until she was kneeling on the bed, the frown deepening. "We're not really married. We wanted to get back at you for leaving us. The kids, all of us." He grew silent as she withdrew completely until she was standing a few feet from the bed.

Charis wrapped her arms about herself. "This was all a... joke?"

Mason sat up, fighting to detangle himself. He looked at her uncomfortably.

"One big joke? Even India?"

"Well... yeah."

"I see."

"We were going to tell you."

"Go."

"Hey, I..."

"Get out..."

"Um, we..."

"Get out!"

He scrambled up. "Maybe I should leave you alone."

"Positively." Her face was closed.

"When is the conference?"

"We really should talk about what happened Charis." India took in her closed face and sighed heavily. "Come on it's been three months, there are people hurting here."

"When is the conference?"

"Damn it all Charis, don't you dare throw it all away!"

Charis looked on in silence. In a fury, India threw the packet she held across her desk. It teetered on the edge. Charis calmly reached out and caught it as it toppled over. "Thank you." She said sarcastically and rose.

India's words halted her at the door. "You're going to be sorry if you let a good thing get away from you twice."

"I do believe that's my choice." She walked away.

Charis sunk against the cool metal wall of the elevator and closed her eyes. Wariness was etched across her face and the elderly couple occupying the space with her looked on in compassion.

As the doors opened, Charis rubbed her brow, attempting to rub away the headache anchored there. When the elevator continued its decent, still her eyes remained closed.

A gentle hand on her cheek had her eyes flying open. "Mason?" Her voice came out in a whisper.

"Hey honey. Headache?" He studied her in concern. "Bad?"

She nodded only to wince from the action. He drew her into his arms. As a "How sweet." was whispered, Charis eyes flew open and she drew back abruptly.

"What are you doing here!" Her voice hardened.

Mason's tone was patient when he spoke. "I know you're a little upset with me and the kids but you really should come home darling."

"I can't believe you." She pushed at his chest but he wouldn't budge. "After all you've done?"

Mason turned to the elderly couple who were all ears. "Our kids, her best friend and I played a silly little prank." The couple smiled understandingly. He turned back to her. "Honey, think of our children if not me."

Charis stared in disbelief. "The children? I don't have any children!"

The couple moved away in shock. Charis looked at them. "I don't have any children, really. He's crazy!"

Mason sighed heavily and reached into the inner pocket of his jacket, drawing out his wallet. "These are our kids. Martin's nine, LaPennie's twelve..."

"LaPennie's thirteen but you wouldn't remember that since you forgot her birthday." Her mouth snapped shut as the couple stared at her. She swallowed. "They're not mine. I'm only the nanny." They looked her over in disbelief. "I mean I was the nanny."

The couple exchanged a look then looked to Mason with compassion. He shrugged sadly before turning back to Charis who was flushed with embarrassment. "Tell them Mason." She tugged on his sleeve.

"What do you want me to tell them sweetheart?"

Charis drew away, eyes flooding with tears. "Why are you doing this to me?" Her voice broke as the tears overflowed.

"Oh Charis." Mason's own voice broke as he drew her into his arms.

Neither noticed when the elevator reached the lobby and the elderly couple looked at them before stepping out. "These young career couples." The man stated as the doors closed.

"What do you mean try an affair?" Mason stormed as he paced the floor.

Charis blushed but held her ground. "I mean we need to see if we're... compatible. I don't even know if I'm ready for a family." She concluded.

Mason whirled about, his face resembling a thundercloud. "It's a bit late for reservations now, you've already got a family... us!"

"No you're not and I won't be forced into marrying you!"

Suddenly Mason was calm. He regarded her silently. "Then that's that." He spoke softly.

A moment later Charis wrapped her arms about herself as she faced the empty suite.

Charis raced frantically through the lobby, tears streaming down her cheeks. "Oh God, please, please!" She whispered brokenly. As she burst through the glass doors she skid to a halt. She clenched her chest, struggling to catch her breath.

"Going somewhere lady?" Unable to speak, she gulped for air. "Wherever you're going you got company." The voice continued.

Charis began to cry harder until she was almost doubled over. Arms drew her back and turned her around. She closed her eyes as Mason drew her up and held her. Her breath caught at his kiss. "Mason?"

"It's okay." He drew her closer. "I was only going for reinforcements. The big guns." He drew her head up and she opened her eyes.

He gestured to a spot behind her. Slowly she turned. "May we go home now madam?" Alvin questioned drily.

Charis looked from Alvin to Annia, her gaze caressed LaPennie and Mason. Her voice caught on a sob. "Yes, lets go home." At her words the kids rushed into her arms.

"Very good madame." Alvin commented. He and Annia exchanged a smile.

As the group moved away, they passed the elderly couple from the elevator. Glancing up, Charis smiled sheepishly as Mason's arm tightened about her. The couple shook their heads and continued past. "Darn kids." The man stated.

His wife pinched his side. "I can remember a time..." She started.

A slow smile crossed his face. He drew her close. "I remember it well." He kissed her.

"Fresh." She accused. "Just the way I like it." She giggled as they moved on eagerly.

No Greater Love

Back in the early 1950's, long before women began to roar or dream of burning their bras, there lived a young woman name Sicily Tucker. Sicily was married to Franklin Horatio Tucker. They had been married for twenty-six years and every day he had the power to make her heart race with a mere look.

As with any other couple there had been hard times such as when he had been laid off from his job at the mill; but being ever faithful and supportive, Sicily had gone to work cleaning houses, taking in laundry and numerous additions she could put her hand to. Strangely, she had not mind at all for she had enjoyed, actually taken great pleasure in being able to help her love.

No one could have been prouder the day he received his Engineering degree. She had refused to allow him to work and attend school but had worked herself so that he could concentrate wholly on his studies. Oh, people had talked but she knew it was all for their future.

Their future was to begin with that special little house. One built just for them that no one else had ever lived in. Their own little piece of heaven on earth. They would have it... as soon as he could get the down payment.

The job had been a blessing. The company which had hired him right out of college was sending him to Okinawa. His job was to reconstruct bridges. Sicily didn't mind for he would only be gone for six months. So her beloved Franklin had gone.

The letters, cards and little gifts had begun to arrive almost immediately. She had written a token protest on his spending so much on her but she had loved it.

The first time he had written about the job being extended she had felt such joy, for surely they would be able to buy their dream house upon his return. Then the letters and trinkets became fewer and fewer, the extensions longer and longer and she had come to regret her token protest.

Soon a year had passed. Sicily looked until she found a new project. Surely she could surprise Franklin upon his return by beginning the house. Of course she knew it would not be completed upon his return but that was quite alright, they could complete it together.

The money she made from her home projects had been placed in the bank since Franklin had finished school. With his departure she had had more time on her hands so she worked even more. She had fairly bubbled over the day she put the down-payment down on the unfinished home. Then she had waited.

One month she had the floors laid, the next the walls, the next, the walls insulated. For six months, bit by bit the house grew closer and closer to completion. When the cost overshadowed her savings she took out a loan for surely with all Franklin was saving they could pay it off upon his return.

Sicily forced herself not to think too long on how scarce the letters had become. Then suddenly a month had passed and Franklin had not written at all. Unable to pay the rent on the apartment and the sweet little house, Sicily moved into the dream.

The little house was a dream home. The yellow paint was the shade which shone cheerfully on the dreariest days. The cookie-cutter shutters brought to mind marshmallows and clouds because of their whiteness.

Two weeks later, she received a letter. The letter was not from Franklin, not directly but rather from a lawyer...in Mexico informing her she was no longer Mrs. Tucker. A week later she received a note from Franklin. His new wife was younger than their marriage... she was nineteen, the daughter of the woman who did his laundry, she was Japanese... her name, Nyang Lee.

Sicily had sat down on her new sofa, the one she had picked just for her beloved Franklin who wasn't hers anymore, in the dream house she had made just for them and reached for the anger and fury within her.

Four years later she still had not found it so she decided to get on with her life. Two weeks later, a second note came. Once again she sat on the sofa, this time she cried. Not for herself but because of the contents of the letter. Her beloved Franklin, for she knew not how to end his being so, had cancer.

Sicily did then what only she could do... she sat down and wrote a final letter, asking Franklin to come home... and bring his wife and the daughter born to them.

As she stood waiting for the passengers to disembark, she grasped her stomach and silently spoke to the knotted nerves, willing peace to them. Slowly they relaxed only for her breathing to halt at the sight of Franklin and the child beside him for surely it had to be a child.

Her gaze took in the toddler holding the childs hand. Nyang Lee came barely to her husband's shoulder, her thinness gave her the child-like appearance. For the first time, Sicily felt something akin to anger.

As the child Nyang Lee hung back in hesitation, Sicily's arms opened. The bird-child flew in and landed in her heart. As the days turned into weeks, into months, the relationship between the two women grew much to the dismay of beloved Franklin.

Sicily became Sissy to Nyang Lee, and Nyang Lee became much to Sicily's dismay, like a daughter. And the child named Lily thrived.

Sicily had tried so to prevent any such attachment to the bird-child, yet the bird continued to return singing her unheard song of enchantment. Quite frequently, the older woman would awaken to find the bird-child perched at the side of her bed fast asleep. Always with one hand outstretched as though to make certain Sicily was still there.

Franklin had not taken to this at all and voices often rang out in the dream house, nevertheless, often Sicily would still awaken to find Nyang Lee curled up on the floor beside her bed.

At one point Franklin appeared on the point of recovery, his anger acting as medication to his weakening body. He had cornered the bird but found to his dismay the bird now had a voice. In response to his command that she stayed away from Sicily, which was difficult living in the same house, the bird had flown at him.

Poor Franklin was void of understanding about how easy it is for love to draw a flower towards the sun. The fear Nyang Lee had at living in a strange country was swallowed up in the love Sicily showed to her and her child. Her behavior had birth in Nyang Lee a hunger to know more about the God who had graced her Sissy with such a warm love.

She had attempted to question Franklin about Sissy's God but his response, "We have the same God." incited her.

"No!" The bird had chirped in anger, "Your God have different rules for male and female. Her God has same rules for all." Franklin had been dumbfounded. From that moment, he had sought diligently to separate the two.

Now Sicily had continued to work as the drama unfolded in her little dream house and little Lily had watched in silence. Day by day the little flower was being drawn to Sissy and try as she might, Sissy could not deny her innocence and freshness. It was not long before they had formed a tight knit family with Franklin on the outskirts.

Month after month they grew closer. Day after day Sicily found herself fighting the desire for once beloved Franklin to depart. How the people talked as people will do. The day Nyang Lee exploded in the grocery store was voiced of from one end of town to the other.

It had come to past like this... Sicily had offered to work late so Nyang Lee had to do what she feared most... shop in an American Supermarket. Franklin drove her. Once inside his patience was tested, and failed as she insisted on meticulously shopping for exactly what Sissy had written. Franklin had almost lost it when she had refused to allow him to place Best flour in the shopping cart because Sissy only used Pillsbury. What would have normally taken ten to fifteen minutes took over an hour and a half.

When Sicily had returned to the dream house it was to find a raging Franklin and she thought again how nice it would be if he left... alone.

Due to her single status, Sicily found herself working most holidays, that included Thanksgiving the following year. Nyang Lee had thought up a way to surprise her mother-sister-friend. She would cook the traditional American holiday meal... and cook it she did just like Sicily had the year before.

Sicily had returned home to find Nyang Lee huddled in the kitchen in tears. Her muffled, "Killed bird for second time." was not understood until she had led Sicily to the oven. Upon opening it, the woman had gasped, then burst into laughter. She then drew the sobbing woman-child in her arms and comforted her as best she could in between laughs.

It took two days for Sicily to clean the turkey off all the oven walls for each time she looked at the mess she would laugh until she cried. From that day forward it would be a family joke that everytime a turkey was prepared the preparer would be cautioned to make certain everything had been removed from inside the bird, for Nyang Lee's act of love had exploded because of this error and the family had sat down to a dinner of chicken and stuffing rather than the turkey which clung to every inch of the oven.

In the second year, Franklin had attempted once again to take Nyang Lee away, but she had used her improving english and hungry mind against him. She had at Sicily's suggestion begun to read and her mind was swift. When Franklin had insisted she move away with him, the bird had screeched, "Sissy my friend, not leave. In America now, I have choice." And so they had stayed.

The next year became a turning point. It was then that Sicily finally gathered enough nerve to approach Franklin and ask the question. Franklin had looked away in shame and sadness but he had given her the answer. "I needed to be needed again. Everything was crazy here. Women's rights, burning bras, there was no telling what they would be burning next. It was nice to see a woman who didn't mind being a woman.

Dressing like a woman and willing to cater to and care for her man."

Sicily had stared at him in confusion. "Isn't that what I was doing?"

He had sighed before hanging his head. "I wasn't first in your life."

"You were."

"No... he was."

"I've never loved anyone but you."

"He was first."

"He... who was he? I didn't..." she had swallowed her words in amazement. "You mean God?"

"I had to be first."

At this Sicily had sighed. "Then it was for the best." She had walked away and the door had finally been closed.

It had not been many days after his confession that Franklin became sick again. This time there was no fight and in less than three months Franklin was not only no longer beloved Franklin... he no longer was. Some say the saying came true... God doesn't like ugly and isn't too impressed with pretty and Franklin had been a bit of both.

At Franklin's passing, the two women discovered he had been saving money all of those years. The account was turned over to Nyang Lee along with the lump sum settlement from his insurance. In all her sweetness she had tried to get her Sissy to take the money. She would not.

But everyone knows real love always finds a way to give. The money sat in the bank for almost a year gathering interest. It was at this time that Sicily found Nyang Lee's stubbornness had not died with Franklin. When Sicily slipped at work and had to take time off, Nyang took great joy in "taking care" of her Sissy. After Sicily recovered and returned to work, once again the money sat. The two would have probably gone on forever as such had not the wisdom of a child stepped forth.

Lily had returned from school and asked the two adults a profound question. "What do you want to be when you grow up?" After that it had been much easier for the two women to come to a compromise.

This tale could go on and on for a new chapter is being written everyday, but I will only tell you this... there have been no exploding turkeys lately. Nyang Lee is in school, she's studying to become an RN. Sicily spends half days teaching english to those studying for their citizenship test, but she makes certain she's home when Lily returns from school. The dream house is filled with dreams and it's all paid in full... curtesy of the once twice beloved Franklin.

The First Time

SWF seeks marriage of convenience. Must own home, business man preferred. Non-smoker, non-drinker. Do not expect duckling to turn into swan. No children now or pending.

"What type of man do you expect to answer an ad like that?" Adonica stared at her best friend. "I know you want out of the house but this is a bit..." She was at a loss for words.

"Desperate is the word you're looking for." Kay supplied.

"Okay, if you know the word, why are you going through with it?"

"Want to go home with me?"

"Not on your life!"

"Point made."

"Do you know what it is you desire?" His voice flowed over her.

"No." She answered honestly.

"Then how will you know when it comes to you?"

She thought for a moment. "I guess I won't... and therefore I shall miss it as I've missed everything else in my life."

"Can I see you?"

"No."

"Why not?"

"I've been here before. People like me until they see me. They don't care for the wrappings."

"Meaning?"

"Meaning if we were to meet you wouldn't be interested. My outside have never measured up to my voice...or me."

"What if I'm not like the rest?"

"You will be."

"How can you be so certain?"

"How can you not?"

He stared at the woman as she came out into the outer office. The receptionist glanced up and smiled. The Fedex man smiled also. "Kay my darling, we've got to stop meeting like this."

"Not as long as you're bringing such great stuff." She shot back jokingly. She took the express packet and signed his board.

"Only for you, only you." He winked, turned and left.

"Anything else Tyra?" She asked the receptionist.

Tyra rose and moved to the mail cubicles behind her. "Nothing much." She handed a pile to Kay with a smile. The man seated silently in the corner of the reception area coughed. Kay turned, giving him a brief glance and smile. "Kay..." she turned back to the young woman. "Will you tell Troy his client is waiting on your way back?"

"Sure." She turned fluidly and moved back to the door. Before she could remove the badge clipped to her belt there was a click as Tyra pressed the release at the desk. Kay glanced back to her. "Thanks." In an instant she was through the security door and moving down the hall.

"Down the hall, third door on the right."

Kay gave the receptionist an absent-minded smile and turned in the direction indicated, missing the curious inspection given her person.

Her heels clicked in rhythm on the beautiful rich mahogany hardwood floor, halting as she reached the door. She took in the gold plate on the door which simply read craig landsing. No title, only his name. "How...refreshing." She thought and knocked.

"It's a shame really."

"Why's that?" Craig turned, staring intently.

"It seems a waste to turn such a beautiful home into an office building."

"Ah-h. Let me show you something." A light hand at her elbow guided her back down the hall.

"Lindsay, take my calls for me. I'll be back in about an hour." The receptionist merely nodded in compliance without glancing from her typing... until they reached the door.

"Well?"

"I've never seen anything like it. To enter on the second floor." She stared in awe at the white marble foyer.

The room was completely open, round and lit seemingly by the sun itself. There were walls of windows which allowed the sun to reflect off the pristine white furniture and silver and glass tables. The openness allowed one to see through to the kitchen which shown regal in glass and stainless steel.

"You don't have any kids do you?"

"Not right now, but I hope to be working on it real soon." She glanced sideways at him, eyebrow raised. "Come on." A light touch at the back of her waist had her obeying.

She stood staring out the glass door. "It's absolutely beautiful. It's just so perfect."

Craig watched her closely. "Despite turning the other one into an office building?"

She laughed self-consciously. "It really is a nice house, not anything like this but still nice."

"I'll remember that."

"There's no reason to, what's done is done."

"Is anything ever really final?"

She glanced at him then quickly turned away. "Only the things that matter most." She turned to look over the room.

"Do you think that'll change or fade?" He nodded towards the yard.

She looked back out the door. "All it would take is a storm."

"Until then it could be enjoyed."

She stood silently for a moment. "Your own private Eden. You can just look out and bask. But..."

He interrupted. "It's privacy glass." There was laughter in his voice. "I know where you were heading, but it's very private. You can see out but no one can see in."

"Ah, well..." She turned and froze. His voice faded away as she stared at the couple on the sofa. The woman was astride the man. Her dress hung down about her forearms. Her head was flung back giving him full access. They moaned as one, absorbed in each other. Kay could faintly hear the soft whispers of their mingled moans as the man continued caressing the womans breast with his mouth.

Kay caught her breath as he raised his head to seize the womans lips. In a daze, she became aware of the womans identity. A sob rose in her throat as she spun around.

Craig's voice came back to her. "What's wrong, talk to me..." He grabbed her arm but she tore it away as though scald.

"I have to go." She moved quickly across the room looking straight ahead.

"Wait." She froze, identifying with the underlaying panic in his voice. She closed her eyes and forced herself to breathe normally. "Before you go at least look at the rest. I'd like you to see it." He reached out, stopping short of touching her arm but she still felt the heat. Kay opened her eyes yet avoided looking directly at him.

The two had just exited the two smaller bedrooms. Where is this heat rising from, she thought. She had to do something, so she spoke. "Bedrooms on the third floor? Isn't that pretty far?"

"For what?"

She turned away slightly embarrassed. "Male and female rooms, that's a nice touch."

"For the children to come."

She looked back at him. "That's terribly optimistic."

"Terribly." He smiled. "And now..." He led her to a much larger room which stretched the full length of the top floor. "This is where the masters dwell."

She moved about the room taking in the rich Victorian bed with its high posts and the marble topped dresser and chest. The floor length windows were covered in willowy white gauze with cascading ivy leaves reaching the floor in its liquid like folds. The white marble fireplace stood on tiger paws with its hearth lined with silver picture frames waiting to be filled.

The ringing of the ivory and gold ornate phone startled her. Craig moved to the side of the bed. "It must be important for the office to put a call through. Look around, I'll only be a minute."

Kay did as instructed. She gasped at the beauty of the porcelain bathroom. The regal setting rivaled the finest hotel suite. The droning of Craig's voice served as a musical undertone as she moved to the closet which lite as she opened the door and revealed itself to be the size of a small bedroom in itself.

Kay's breath caught as she examined the inside. The length of one side was packed with obviously expensive womens clothes, everything from jeans to evening wear. The shelf above held a variety of accessories. The far wall housed enough shoes to stock a small store front shop.

Kay sucked in her breath in panic. Craig jerked about in surprise as she fled the room. He caught up with her at the stairs. "Let me go, let me go!" She cried.

"Tell me what's wrong."

"Let me go!"

"Please, just tell me what's wrong." He pleaded. She turned away from the heat in his eyes.

"I want to go... now." She could feel the heat of his · gaze on her face.

"We'll go down now." He took care not to release her completely.

Kay forced herself not to pull away and run though the very desire to do so caused her body to tremble.

Her heart raced as they descended the stairs and reached the door. Craig placed his hand on the door knob and stood still.

"Please." She whispered.

"Stay." He whispered. Her eyes closed in pain. "Please stay with me." He whispered without looking at her. He swallowed, voice thick. "I built it for you. I brought the clothes, planned everything just for you. I've waited over a year to get you here, don't leave me now."

He turned, tears in his eyes. "What are you so afraid of?"

"I don't understand."

"And I don't understand what frightens you so. What did you see in that room?"

Kay turned away and stood hugging herself. "What do you mean you did it all for me?"

"Lets go in the family room." Kay hesitated then wrapping her arms tighter about herself she moved towards the room. Craig trailed her slowly.

Once there he gestured to the sofa but silently shaking her head she moved to stand before the glass doors.

"It's a bit unbelievable but just hear me out."

"I'm listening... for now."

"I saw you in a dream." He began. She turned to face him. "I don't know why or how, I only know I did. Then when I dialed that number over a year ago and you were at the other end. It was fate."

"It was a wrong number."

"But it became more."

She turned away again. "I was crazy."

"And I was desperate to hear from you again."

"You kept calling."

"I had to. Our conversations became the center of my life. I'd call you from work, anything to hear your voice. Then when you would never agree to meet me, I felt my world had fallen apart."

"How did you come by the office. I never told you where..."

"Things you said. Little clues I picked up on. I had to see you and I didn't have any other way. I could have gotten someone else to deliver that proposal but it was an opportunity I couldn't pass."

"You recognized me? How?"

"From the dream, and I'd know your voice anywhere."

Kay finally relaxed. "The receptionist was impressed. She spoke of you for days."

"Really?" He made his way cautiously to her side. "What did you think?"

For a moment she didn't respond. "I tried not to."

"Did you succeed?" He asked hopefully.

"Not very." She confessed. Craig chuckled in relief. "Am I here under pretense?"

His laughter froze. "I didn't know any other way to get you here."

She turned to stare at him. "Does everyone know... about all of this?"

"No. The contracts were real, I just had them faxed as soon as you got to the office. My secretary called and told them there was a delay, a problem with your car. As for my office, yes they know."

"Why?"

"Because I had to tell someone."

"I'm sure I can imagine what they think."

"I'm sure you can't." There was silence. "So will you stay?"

"For how long?"

"I won't ask for forever but how about forever minus a week?"

"No one will ever believe this?"

"Does it matter?" He drew her into his arms and released a sigh of relief.

She wrapped her arms timidly about his neck. "No, I guess not." She whispered.

"So you'll stay?" He nuzzled her neck.

"Only until a week before forever." She buried her head in his chest.

"I'll take it if that's all I can get." He held her in silence for a moment and she held him back. Suddenly his brow wrinkled and he drew back to look in her eyes. "What was it that frightened you in here?" For a moment she lowered her head. "Please tell me."

Kay raised her head and allowed herself to be warmed by the concern there. Taking him by the hand she drew him across to the sofa as she whispered, "I'll show you."

Nappy And Me: Through The Storm

Before the police could find all of Mirtle's body parts the beauty parlors were filled with women preparing to console Jimmy, her grieving widower. Now everyone was sadden by the untimely not to mention unsightly demise of Mirtle but as in all small southern towns, life went on in Coltrane County.

Were you to question any of Mirtle's many friends which spanned thirty to forty years, they would all speak of two things. One would be her love of tidiness which was her downfall. You see, it was her compulsive habit of picking up trash which led to her stopping to pick up what appeared to be an empty paper bag from the street. The contents of which sent her flying in different directions at the same time. Friends would also speaking in glowing terms of her luck at having such a wonderful husband, that is as they peered around you to get a look at the object of that very phrase.

The funeral drew more participants than the club, the pool hall and even the church social, though in reality you couldn't tell the difference by appearance. Between the flow of tears one could witness the subtle and not so subtle art of courtship in play.

The women, those proficient in the maneuver, made certain their Sally-made hats remained on their heads as they 'fainted', that is those fortunate enough to be standing near an unattached male. It was a perfect ploy for what man would allow a woman to hit the ground? Unfortunately the hero would often find himself unable to dislodge the damsel and found himself in distress when she came to. I didn't participate for two reasons: One, I was too young; and two, I was too busy praying for a friend.

The excitement of Mirtle's funeral pushed my own problems from the front page of our nonexistent newspaper. But that very same excitement did nothing to distract Nappy from her goal... to answer my prayer with or without my permission. A quick note; they never found who was responsible for the bomb which speeded Mirtle on her way , besides something else drew their attention you see the mad bomber as we came to call him... or her had their sights on a bigger target. They blew up the chicken plant the next weekend which was the 4th of July.

Nappy entered my life the day I was born; I was eight years old. She was the friend no one wanted, yet everyone needed. She was the fired breath of a nightmare during the day and the gentle candy-coated angel's kiss at night. In herself she was my beginning and with every whispered prayer, I expected her to be my end. It was Nappy who taught me if you really wanted to know a person, to visit their bathroom for it was within those walls that numerous secrets were revealed.

Nappy first appeared after IT happened. In the beginning Mama thought she was a hallucination brought on by IT. That was until Nappy moved in. Even now I am hard pressed to speak of IT but I will say the man was never found, it is something most young girls fear in small towns were every man is considered their uncle.

Anyway, back to Nappy. I know the images her name brings to mind but disregard them please. She was as tall as she was skinny, her skin very pale and her hair very, very red. It was such a shade of red that if one got too close they swore they could feel heat.

If Nappy had a family of her own we never knew of them. No one knew where she'd come from nor when she would see fit to leave. After a time, she just became one of us and no one thought about it much; at least not directly to us. There were some who chose to talk behind our backs even when our backs weren't turned; yet we pretended not to hear even though our ears were wide open.

Nappy also succeeded as nothing else could in putting to rest a bad habit I held dear. In my life I was forever people watching and measuring myself by what I saw. And the scales were forever tilted in the other persons favor.

She made me look beyond the outer covering: the nice clothes and prestigious job, the circle of affluent friends. It did not take much for me to look away. Actually, it took only one visit to my idols home and a few brief moment alone in her bedroom.

You know, dresser drawers reveal a lot too. My idol was held together by safety pins and hastily applied green nylon thread. I could not fathom how one who took such pains to look good on the outside via expensive clothes, would be content with undergarments which wouldn't stand up to the light of day or as Nappy says, "Couldn't survive the scrutiny of the washline on the other side of the tracks."

Yes, Nappy was my confidant and my teacher. My lessons took place in the classroom called life and I never knew when there would be a pop quiz; even my exams were unscheduled.

When I tried to stand on my own I often had to face my giants over again, but when Nappy guided me I only had to face them once.

The name Nappy was first presented by my Aunt Mayme. My aunt was what the old folks called, "Light, bright and darn near white." Many saw this as a blessing but Aunt Mayme saw it as a curse and she had the stories to back her opinion.

Anyhow, one day at the beginning of my family's acceptance of Nappy, my aunt attempted to tame the rebellious red hair. She lost the battle but not before branding the child for life. I can still hear the frustration in her voice as she declared, "It doesn't make no kind of sense a child with a head this nappy."

Years later the hair would grow out and become tamed waves, (on a good day), yet the name remained. There are many events which colored our youth with deep palettes of gray. I yet remember the day the social worker Mrs. Gladys came to the house to take Nappy away. Social Services was very uncomfortable with the idea of a white child growing up in a black household, (this was in the day when it was okay to be called black). Never mind that no one else would claim her. It just wasn't 'proper'. No one was willing to acknowledge it was the mammies of old who raised all the masters children.

Times really haven't changed. We hear of numerous cases where children are being taken from their homes on the whim of officials and political groups who believe it is unhealthy for them to grow in certain environments. There are the black children taken from white homes for fear they will not know what it means to be black when they grow up. (I wonder if perhaps none of these households have mirrors.)

I personally find it strange that it is only with a black child that it is necessary for them to learn how to be what they are. Does an Indian, Asian or even white child have to learn how to be what they are? There are also cases of white children being taken from loving homes for fear they will... become black maybe? But nevertheless...

Anyhow, Mrs. Gladys had sought diligently to find a white family to take Nappy but none came forth. It was then decided that she would be placed in an orphanage rather than remain where she was.

We were to learn much later, two years to be exact, that my parents fought to keep Nappy with us. Though they never spoke of it, they too had grown rather attached to the 'strange' child as they were so fond of calling her around the neighbors. I should have known this was the case when Christmas presents just happened to show up out of nowhere with her name on them. The extra stocking with the embroidered name was a dead give away.

It was a sad day for us all when Mrs. Gladys came for Nappy. No one could meet anyone else eyes for fear of showing and seeing tears. Only the star of the day was herself. There was one difference in her that day as I now recall. It could only be described as anticipation. It was as though she had information no one else was party to.

The entire extended household walked outside with Nappy. We stood on the porch like tin soldiers commanded not to desert their post under penalty of death. There was no touching. Mrs. Gladys kept her body between us and Nappy as though she was the dividing line which separated the offensive from the defensive team, or perhaps the North from the South.

As they entered the big black automobile, neither bothered to look back. The pain of that cut so deep my own tears froze instantly. I vaguely felt a hand drawing me to a body bigger than my own, offering me warmth and a bit of comfort. We watched as they drove off. All I could see was the back of that forest of red curls.

When the dust settled we were inside standing dumbly about the living room. My tears quickly unthawed. You see, unconditional love is a dangerous thing, it can be shaken but never recalled.

I stood with head bowed and tears flowing, still no one spoke. It was as though a death had taken place and no one knew what to say. Suddenly, a knowing came over me. It was nothing I could explain or voice, I could only react and react I did. The room became a blur as I swung about and raced back towards the porch. As I burst through the front door I came to an abrupt halt. There just inside the yard stood our Nappy, suitcase at her side, the one grandma Moses had given her, and a smile as old as time upon her slightly crooked lips.

I was unaware that my family had quickly pursued me as I exited, nor was I aware of them standing behind me. As though the move had been carefully choreographed we turned as one to glance up the road. Disappearing in a cloud of dust was Mrs. Gladys car. From that moment till now, we have never heard from Mrs. Gladys or social services again. The mystery remains unsolved about what happened to this day. By way of silent agreement we never asked. The old folks just said, "The Lord works in mysterious ways".

After that life just seemed to go on for Nappy and me. Sometimes like a steady rainfall which teased beautiful flowers into coming out and showing their new wardrobes, others violent hurricane winds which picked us up and flung us into the next chapter of our destines.

Nappy would go forth eyes open, embracing the winds while my own would be tightly shut as I fought to cling to the roof shingles.

Nappy had a magician's timing, in that she knew how to appear when I needed her and disappear when all was well. Now I don't want you to misunderstand and think she was perfect, she wasn't perfect, she just... was.

I'll never forget during my college years when she brought her first car. It was a little bug. I remember she had bought it real cheap. It was a stick, the only problem with that was Nappy didn't know how to drive a stick. But being Nappy, she found a way to deal with that too.

She calmly asked the Salesman to start the car and turn it in the right direction (that was pointing to the street) and she just took off down the hill. She said so long as she could get it to stop and go they would be just fine.

I believe many a people talked to God when they found themselves either in front of or behind Nappy... whether they believed in him or not.

There were two things Nappy hated with a passion as hot as her hair: profanity and mediocrity. The one was a sign of its users need to continue schooling to enable them to find words to describe what they felt. The other was playing God cheap. She would always say, "God made you an original why be a copy? Besides, mediocre is harder to spell." So I continued my education and never used profanity.

Nappy claims I got all those degrees not to learn new words but so I could wallpaper the nursery. See, my husband wasn't too interested in a highly educated woman. (Or maybe it was just he wasn't interested in me). Nappy says it's all a part of the home study course, people are constantly learning everyday of their lives trying to get that big degree. They never know if they graduated until that great white throne judgement but by then you can't make up any classes you may have missed. Yes I had a number of degrees so I guess one would say I was or am well educated. The problem is, when you forget to use your wings once you get them you often forget how to fly. In my case degrees did not help me in learning how to cope with a husband who refused to dream much less be a part of my dreams.

All of this came home to roost the day my divorce was final. I came out of the courthouse in a daze. It's sad how soon you can want to live without the one you couldn't live without, or how I never knew how suddenly a marriage aimed to last "till death do us part" can end with one still living, or at least breathing.

To prove I was indeed still breathing I stopped on the steps to listen to my heartbeat. It was there... barely. As I went down I remember spotting one of those sidewalk vendors. You know, the ones over-priced but it was just the nostalgia which kept them in business.

I ordered a hot dog with everything, after all if I was still alive I had to eat. As I dug into my purse a hand came past me, then an arm. Turning, I knew what was attached to the other end. A matching hand took mine and I allowed myself to be lead away like a child. Can't remember to this day whether or not I got that hotdog. All I knew was Nappy had appeared again and everything was bound to be alright in my little world.

Yes, throughout my life Nappy was the source or at the very least instigator of my greatest pain and deepest pleasure. She took me farther than I wanted to go, made me stay longer than I wanted to stay, care more than I wanted to care and love deeper than I wanted to love.

Its been many years since I last saw Nappy but I know in my knower that should things ever get unbearable in my life again, she'll walk back in just like she walked out. When I need her to show up the most, she'll come. No matter how old I get, she will always be Nappy to me, my mysterious but constant friend and she will return. I know, because that's my Nappy.

The Bag's...
A Lady

I can't believe this, what I am about to share with you is... out of the ordinary. You could say it is beyond extraordinary and be absolutely correct. When I was young, not to say that I'm old, I use to dream of Cinderella. Remember that fairy tale? This poor sweet girl wore rags and had a horrible home life, until her fairy godmother appeared and turned her life into this fantastic reality. All right, so that was a condensed version.

Who would have ever conceived that I had a fairy godmother... of sorts. She was a New York City baglady with a heart of gold. Or was she? I'll tell you my story and you decide. I recall first seeing Paris one day as I rushed off to work. Paris, what a name for a baglady right?

Maybe I should backtrack a little. Allow me to introduce myself. My name is Heartina Johnson. Okay, so my mother was in a romantic mood when I was born. I am twenty-four years of age. I reside in New York City. Times Square to be exact. I realize people are going to ask, "How can you live in Times Square?" Well, there's a little place not too many have had the pleasure of becoming familiar with called the Times Square Motor Hotel. This is the type of place one stays when Holiday Inn and other places of this caliber are beyond their means.

At the time I worked at Bronkey Photo Studio. I was a film technician. It was not as nice as it sounded. All day I sat at a table and cut and load the same film. If that wasn't enough, it was mainly military training films which they show to the new recruits when they join the service.

I should know, I saw the same film about four years ago when I joined the Army. Yes I served four years as a soldier. I can't say that it was an experience I would want to repeat. Anyway that's enough about me for now, allow me to return to my... experience.

I recall first noticing Paris as I was rushing off to work. At the time, I didn't know her name, nor when she had first appeared on the block. I can't even remember why I noticed her at all. For anyone who has ever been to New York you have seen plenty of bagladies. I proceeded to work.

The next day I saw her again. I remember it was rather chilly and she was sitting against the edge of the building with her bags around her, huddled in what you could loosely describe as a coat. Very loosely.

As I was walking past she looked up and smiled. I found myself returning the smile. I stopped and found myself pulling out my change purse, you see I didn't often have need of a wallet because there wasn't too much to put in one. I had three dollars to last me until payday. That day was Monday, payday would be that Friday. I figured I was all right, I had more than enough peanut butter and jelly to last me until then. I gave her the three dollars and told her to get some breakfast. Her smile was beautiful and it made me feel warm, so much so that I didn't notice the chill of the wind as I continued on to work... well almost didn't notice.

All through the day, I kept seeing that smile. The warmth I had felt rather ambled away after my supervisor informed me there was the possibility of a layoff. As it goes, the last person to be hired was the first to go. Take a wild guess at who had been the last one hired, go ahead.

As you can probably guess I was not in the greatest of moods when I returned to the hotel. As I started to mount the stairs I was halted by a slight touch on my arm. I glanced around to see my baglady as I found myself thinking of her. Before I could speak she held out her hand. In it was some change.

I found myself smiling once more. Here was a lady who lived on the streets giving me change when I knew she was in need of it herself. "Go ahead and keep it, you can use it for coffee."

"You can use it for bread."

Can you picture a baglady telling you something like that? As it were she was speaking the truth, but I wasn't about to let her know I had just remembered that. Somehow the money was in my hand and I turned to prevent her from seeing me smile. I tell you, I had smiled more that day then I had in the last four months. As I turned back to her it was to find she was no longer there. I shook my head and went on to my room. It wasn't much of a room but it was home until I made my first million... or at least enough to move someplace better.

I can't recall doing too much of anything that night except watching a MacGyver rerun on television. I went to sleep dreaming of my fashion debut. I was the toast of the town, that was until the alarm went off and awakened me to the real world.

As I went on my way I watched for my baglady, but I wasn't to see her that morning. I couldn't help feeling a little bit disappointed. Upon arriving at work I found that a possibility had become reality. The layoff was to begin the following day. I guess one good thing came out of it. Payday was to be earlier than usual. We were to pick up our checks the following morning.

The day rather dragged on. I began to feel that things weren't meant to get any better. First I hadn't seen my baglady, then I was practically fired. It didn't help to be told to "hang loose" for a week or two, for then they would be rehiring... maybe. What was I to do for those two weeks? What if the maybe didn't turn into a definite? I didn't think for a moment that the hotel would be happy were I to tell them to hang loose for a week or two when it was time to pay my rent.

To add to everything else it began to rain just as I was leaving the office. Things were looking so bad to me, I had no choice but to laugh to prevent myself from crying. I started to think maybe if I could find my baglady she could teach me the ropes and I could become one myself.

By now it had really started to pour. Turning the corner of the hotel I saw her. My baglady was back. And she was soaked. Her bags were covered with plastic and once again sat in a circle around her. After everything else, I couldn't take it. I guess you could say I had a lapse of some sort. Without saying a word I grabbed as many bags as I could carry and left her to follow with the rest. I didn't know whether she would or not. I can't imagine the sight the two of us made as we lugged everything in. I was not to know that this would be the turning point in my life, though looking back I guess I should have known something was up.

Not a word was spoken as we made our way to the elevator and up to my room. It wasn't much as I've said before but at least it was warm and dry. Upon entering, I set her bags on the floor near the radiator. I looked back to find her studying the room. I found myself forced to speak. "It's not much but it's home."

"You have taste. Not fully developed, but taste nevertheless."

"I'm glad you approve. Put your bags down and take off your... coat."

"Why?"

One word, one question yet it was a loaded one. I found myself stuck for an answer. Never before had I just taken a person in, much less off the streets but for some reason I didn't feel she belonged there. Finally I came up with a great answer. "It's raining."

"If you say so." It appeared as though she knew my reason better than I did and she wasn't telling. In my present state of mind I felt anything was possible.

"The bathroom is down the hall. Here's the key, you need to take a shower and change out of those wet clothes." I started to feel like a mother hen. And secretly I liked it, I rather enjoyed being able to boss someone around finally... or so I thought.

When I reentered the room it was to the smell of warm soup. While I had showered and changed my baglady had prepared dinner. On my budget I lived basically on soup, peanut butter and jelly with a few other inexpensive items mixed in for a very limited but much needed variety.

"I'm going to shower, watch the potatoes make sure they don't burn." I spoke not a word as she took the key out of my hand. First let me explain, I guess you have figured out at this point that my bossing didn't quite work. It had something to do with the look she gave me. It reminded me of the looks my mother use to give when she expected me to do something asap. Secondly, about the keys. In rooms such as the one I was fortunate enough to have, you have a bed, sink in the corner, and... and that's it. The bathroom is located down the hall and you have a key to it. This assures the hotel that the only ones who use the community bathroom are the special guests of the establishment.

Being in the Army did teach me one good thing, well actually two. One, how to pack much into a small space, and two, never to join again. I had invested in a small toaster oven, a two-burner hotplate, electric skillet and a small refrigerator. They had survived the Army, my two years in California and now were with me like trusted friends in New York. A little note, upon leaving the military I attended college, Fashion college that is, in California. Okay so I never graduated. I did go for an entire month. I'm a fashion designer. The world just isn't aware of it yet. Upon leaving California I moved to New York.

I had taken the potatoes from the oven and was making toast when she returned. I was rather tired of calling her my baglady but before I could ask her name, she supplied it.

"The name's Paris Ane L'Anglais."

"I'm..."

"Heartina, I know."

"How do you..." Once more I was not allowed to continue.

"Lets eat before the food gets cold." I was to find that I was never to be allowed to have the last word.

As I climbed the stairs I couldn't help wondering how long it would be before I found myself coming down the same with all my worldly possessions. I was about to enter the elevator when I was called over to the main desk by the clerk on duty.

"Excuse me Ms. Johnson, there's a slight problem with your room." The way things were going my mind turned to the worst scenario. "May I have your keys please?"

"Whatever for?"

"There was a break in the radiator. Don't worry, nothing was damaged. Everything has been transferred to the new room." I gave him my room key. "The bathroom key." I turned over that key also. I was rather afraid to go to the new room. Paying one hundred dollars a week in Manhattan, you learn not to expect too much. I had been fortunate in the fact that rarely had I visitors of the four or more legged variety.

At the elevator I looked at the key I now held. Room 1112, my old room had been 905. At least I was moving up in the world. I noticed I had only been given one key. As I turned to go back to the front desk, the elevator arrived. I decided to see the room then return later to get the bathroom key.

Upon reaching the room I found myself holding my breath as I opened the door. The pain in my chest served to remind me that I was still holding my breath minutes later as I stood inside the doorway in a daze. The first thing to enter my mind was that it was a mistake. The second was I couldn't pay for it, for I stood in the doorway of a real room.

"Don't just stand there. Close your mouth and the door while you're at it."

As I moved to obey one word fell from my lips, "Room."

"That's very observant of you."

A few moments later I could say two words, "Can't afford."

"They're charging you the same as what you paid for that broom closet." I could only stare. "They're fully booked, this was the only room left." After years of living in tiny living spaces I was unprepared for all the space I had now been allotted. "Sit down Tina and relax. You're not going to be kicked out tomorrow." Paris smiled. Honestly, I didn't think that. I was thinking more like later on that same night. "Lay down a few minutes while I fix dinner."

I found myself doing as I was told, it was the easiest thing to do. I was still in shock. My having no job was pushed to the back of my mind, momentarily. I was tired. As my head touched the pillow my last thought was: no more sleeping head to foot. You see, the night before with there only having been one bed Paris and I had shared. When I was a child and the relatives visited, most often we had to share beds, therefore we had to sleep with every other person turned the opposite way. It wasn't so bad if the person next to you was short. That way you didn't end up with feet in your face.

Delicious aromas and a light touch on my cheek served to awaken me. I looked up to find Paris smiling down at me. I put the fact that there was a bright glow around her down to my eyes being filled with sleep and were seeing things and forgot about it. "Freshen up and come to the table." Out of habit I headed for the outside door. "The other way." I had forgotten, I was now in a real room. Whereas my closet had only held a sink in the corner this room had a full size true-to-life bathroom. I stood on the threshold. "You use the little knobs with the H and C on them." I heard Paris laughing from across the room. It was the first time I had heard her laugh. The only way to describe it was musical.

For the first time I turned and really looked at Paris. I noticed that I could not began to tell her age. Though her hair was shining silvery-white, her face was ageless as were the sparkling moss-green eyes. There appeared a light in her face as though she were lit from within. Though slightly shorter than my own five feet seven, she appeared not so much stately but regal. She carried herself not as you picture your everyday street person, nor for that matter everyday person, but rather more like a dancer. There was a gracefulness around her even with her wearing worn clothing. I could close my eyes and picture her in Givenchy or Saint Laurent. I just knew she would wear them well. I also knew without a doubt that she should not have been on the street. And herein laid the beginning of my personal battle had I but known.

I don't know for certain but I think sometimes God and his angels sit around heaven and laugh at the antics of his children. I'm almost certain that on this particular day they were having a field day watching my reactions. I could almost hear them. "Hey Gabe, pass me the angel salt for the heavenly popcorn. Hurry up Mikey, she's about to notice something else."

Coming out of the bathroom I just knew I had one, died and was on my way to heaven. Or two, was dreaming. Either way I was hoping I could eat before anything happened. It had been awhile since I had been able to enjoy the smell of steaks broiling. Being the honest type person I am, another word is scared, I attempted to come up with a way to ask Paris a very important question. Before I could come up with a way she supplied the answer.

"I did not steal them. A friend, the butcher from the market gave them to me."

Of course I believed her. You would have had to see Paris, one look and you'd realize that this was one woman who did not lie. I can tell you I breathed a sigh of relief. Paris wouldn't get in trouble and we wouldn't have to give the steaks back. I'm not completely certain at that point which was the most important to me. Being honest, peanut butter and jelly grows stale after awhile. Besides, I didn't want to push this honesty thing too far.

My days went by in this vein for about three or four days. Each day it seemed something new appeared. Simple things such as fresh flowers. Things that in themselves are of no importance to the average person but which makes a great difference to someone like the two of us. Every time I would notice something new Paris would just smile. After the second or third day I stopped asking about the new additions.

By this time my mind had turned to more pressing problems. What were we to do in two days when my rent was due once more? I rather felt as a mother must feel who has a child yet nowhere to go. I worried about what would become of Paris. We had adjusted so well to being together. I didn't know how to tell her that in a few days she would be back on the street and probably me with her.

The day before the rent was due, I found myself with no time left to make my decision and still no job. Should I use the money I had remaining to pay rent or to purchase a bus ticket and return to my mother? My stomach churned at the latter solution. That night I knew I would have to speak to Paris, for my final decision would not effect only myself but her also. I tried to bring the subject up gently ; by now you probably have started to know Paris.

Rather abruptly she confronted me. "Well, are you going to stay and fight or sound retreat?" She was not subtle.

In the face of such a direct attack, how was I to respond? Well, I came up with something really brilliant. "What are you talking about?"

Again I received what I had come to call the I-know-more-than-you-know smile. "Are you going to stay or are you going to run back to mama?"

This time I couldn't pull off pretending not to know what she was referring to. Allow me to explain once again. In my time in New York my mother had sought to persuade (demand) that I return to the city of my birth (and should she have her way, death). To her, drawing pretty pictures of clothing was no way to make a living. Sewing was for making a nice wardrobe, it was not a real job. It was to help you look good for a ... real job.

"Well anyhow, Paris was by this time staring rather intently at me, waiting for an answer. Once again she was... gentle. "Either you give up your dreams and die or you don't and be willing to fight." Nice easy choices wouldn't you say?

I decided to try a different tactic, the one I had been using wasn't working very well. "So Paris what do you think I should do?"

"Go for it." Remember now, she's a lady of few words.

I smiled but then intellect took over. Do you really want to take the advice of a lady who lived on the street? It took me only seconds to answer intellect. After the great job you've done, anything could be an improvement. Therefore it was settled, I paid for another weeks rent and prayed for a job. Up in heaven someone started shouting to the others. "Hey, she finally realized she couldn't do it without help!" And a mighty cheer went up.

I must admit I was not feeling too feisty right about then, you see I'm pretty good at making decisions... the wrong ones. As it happens, I went to a temporary job agency, you know the ones which say, "Join us and work only when you want to." I was ready to work, they weren't. After spending three hours taking test after test to register, I was informed they would call if any work came in. Jobs were coming in rather slow.

Trying not to allow my desperation to show, I drew on my coat and headed for the door. Just as I opened it and the frigid air blew in I heard one of the counselors call out, "You wouldn't happen to be interested in an assistant designer position would you?"

Let me tell you, my heart dropped out of my body. The only thing which prevented it from hitting the floor was my right boot. I could feel it pumping in the toe section. I was otherwise calm and once again brilliant. "Huh?" I could have sworn the counselor was trying not to laugh.

"We have to fill a assistant designer position at a fashion house but haven't been able to find anyone the head designer likes. Would you happen to know anyone who may be interested in trying, we're desperate."

"I know the feeling well." In New York everyone wants to be an artist, actor, model or designer and they were having a hard time finding one?

"Excuse me?"

"What are the qualifications?" Was that really me asking questions?

"Basic design knowledge, sewing, good attitude, fast learner..." She was definitely speaking my language. "Associate degree..." Oh-oh, trouble ahead. "Negotiable." Backtrack, rewind.

"The degree is negotiable?"

"Yes, they want someone who is willing to learn from the bottom up, but who has the basics."

Don't blow it now. "How basic?"

"Does this mean you're interested?"

You're really fast on the uptake. "Yes."

"Come into my office."

Half an hour later I had an appointment the following morning. By the time I reached the hotel, I just knew people were running around looking for one of those white jackets with the sleeves in backwards. It wasn't my fault that I couldn't stop smiling at everyone on the street.

Riding the elevator, I couldn't wait to tell Paris what had happened. Bursting in the door, I was overcome by the aroma which attacked me. "Come in and close the door child, you're letting the heat out." Quickly I did as I were told. It wasn't until after our dinner of trout, broccoli with cheese sauce and corn, that I remembered to tell her the great news. As I spoke, she said not a word. I just knew she was going to remind me that at this point I did not have the job. I knew wrong.

Paris stood and walked over to the closet. Opening it she withdrew what she considered to be my best designs. While I had been job hunting, she had taken the time to unpack my trunk and iron all my design samples. I now had nicely pressed samples to take to my appointment. She had also taken out my portfolio and dust it off. You see, I was one of those people who gave up on their dreams. I was too much of a coward to throw them away, but I didn't work on them either. I only dreamed. Looking me in the eye she gave me some words of wisdom. "Beauty and dreams were never meant to be hidden, nor forgotten. The dream without the drive will only get you as far as you are now."

I was astonished, I was also staring to wonder about this lady I was sharing my life with. I soon found that this was indeed my night and I had another surprise in store. Seated on the bed glancing through my portfolio,

I looked up to find Paris standing before me holding out sheets of paper.

"Fill them out." No questions, no explanations. I looked down to find I held admission and financial aid forms for the community college. "Classes start in two weeks, you have time to register."

I was deeply touched that she had gone through the trouble to try and help me and I told her so. "Thank you Paris, that was sweet of you." Now for the let down. "Unfortunately I can't afford to take any classes right now." I figured I had handled that quite well... wrong.

"There is such a thing as financial aid. I'm certain you've heard of it before."

"It's pretty late to apply..."

"Apply." It was not a suggestion. I did what any other adult taking care of themselves would have done in my position... I shut up and filled out the forms.

I was nervous the next day when I arrived for my appointment. As I sat in the reception area, I sent up some pretty heavy prayers. Let me tell you, I don't know the formal forms people use when they pray. I've never been very good at making it all sound impressive. My prayer went like this; Lord, it's me. Know it's been awhile but if you're not super busy I could really use some help. A job would be really nice right about now. By the way, thanks for Paris and the great food this past week. Oops, excuse me Lord, they're calling me... do you mind going first? I'm right behind you.

Have you ever met a person for the first time and hated yourself for liking them? That was how I felt about Aja Kantrell. Exotic sounding and it matched her looks. It was down right disgusting. She could have just stepped out of a high fashion magazine. Long wavy hair the color of autumn leaves, auburn yet golden. Sparkling hazel eyes, complexion the color of creamy caramel and a smile that would light up all of New York City in a blackout.

I could feel myself shrinking in her presence. It hurt to look at her but I couldn't prevent myself from doing so. I was barely aware of answering her questions. In a daze my portfolio and resume exchanged hands. As though from a great distance I heard her instruct me to follow. I seem to recall being led to other offices but I have no memory of what I saw or why. I didn't come into full awareness of my surroundings until I found myself shaking hands with Aja.

"So we'll see you tomorrow and welcome aboard." I blinked. "Are you okay?"

"I have the job?" Genius at work here.

She laughed. "Of course, that's why you had the tour. Don't worry, we'll show you around again."

Seeing her smile I knew I couldn't pretend any longer. "I'm sorry, I..."

"I know you don't remember any of it."

"What gave me away?"

"When you shook hands with the doorknob." I could feel myself drowning in a wave of embarrassment. "It's okay, it'll be better tomorrow, see you at eight." I still wasn't immune to that smile but at least it didn't hurt as much. As I turned to leave her office Aja called out, "Welcome to G.O. Incorporated, I think this is going to be a new beginning for you."

I paused. "Do you know, in the past week I've had a lot of those?" This time I returned her smile with one of my own and you know what? I don't think it was half bad.

The next two weeks passed in a blur. It was as though my entire existence had taken a new and wondrous direction and for the first time, I was enjoying... life. Miracle upon miracle I had a nice place to stay, a wonderful roommate, great job, (I didn't have to be concerned about paying rent because payday was every friday and I was paid the first week due to the finance office being in the company building), not to mention what a challenge it was. On top of this, I found myself attending school nights. I had been pleasantly surprise to find that not only had I received a nice size grant, (a benefit of making very little money), but also a partial scholarship. If that wasn't enough to put a person on cloud nine, G.O. Incorporated supplemented me. In the company if you attended school and took classes which enhanced your job performance, you received an extra bonus.

Things were going so great I should have known trouble was right around the corner. Trouble was five foot eleven inches, had reddish-blonde hair, green-grey eyes and went by the name Trevor Donnely. He was gorgeous, masculine and powerful in a lean sort of way. He was long of limb and sinewy. Broad of shoulder, narrow of waist and standing on my foot.

At the time I couldn't see having made a good impression on him, for a woman hopping on one foot has never been listed in Cosmo as one of the ten unforgettable meetings.

A month went by, between settling in at G.O. and school three times a week, I was in heaven, at least as close as you could get on earth. Aja started laughing at me one day. She couldn't understand how I could be so excited with small things such as picking up pins in the design studio.

After years of not seeing your dreams come any closer, it doesn't take much to excite you when you can see them materializing. Aja was definitely one of the nicest people I had ever met. During my first month with her, we became very close. I learned a lot about her own life. It was not all a pretty picture.

Aja became my mentor. You have to respect a person who has fought for their future against the odds. I had always believed that when you are beautiful, life is easier for you than the average person. Through Aja, I learned differently. One night while dining with her and her family, I made a vow to myself to make her proud of me. You see, Aja was one half of an interracial couple. She had, with her husband fought the courts for custody of his daughter. It had not been easy but they had triumphed. They never gave up. Who could ask for a better example of courage and determination?

Anyhow life was fantastic. My only concern was Paris. I didn't get to see her very often. Just when I was starting to go soft she attacked. "When are you going to get a life?" With a single question, she had done it yet again. She had completely thrown me off balance. Here I was in a position I had always dreamed about;

great job, going to school, a roof over my head that didn't leak. Look, I even had a bank account that wasn't in over draft. What more could a girl want?

"You should have a young man." That was what more. You know me, being the honest person I am, I... told Paris of all I did have. Okay, so it's known as justification. Politicians do it all the time, why couldn't I? It was bound to work. I mean I didn't want to be greedy. So many people didn't have all that I did. It would work right? Wrong.

"Why shouldn't you have it all?" Yeah, why shouldn't I? "Don't you think you're worth it?" Of course... didn't I? "There are plenty of people out there who have more than average, why shouldn't you be one of them? Why just settle for medium?" That's right. "So what are you going to do about it?" Oh-oh, trick question. "Isn't there anyone your age at work, or school?" Time out, danger ahead. Visions of green-grey eyes swam across my eyes. "Well?" The vision shattered. "Heartina..."

Avoidance maneuver ahead. "Paris I'm too busy right now for a relationship."

"A relationship with the right person is an enhancement to one's life not an inconvenience." Hey, give me credit, I tried. This woman was a pro.

What came next I could safely blame on Paris. Every school night I found myself looking for the toe-stomper... Trevor. As it were, I didn't have to look hard or far. It appeared we were always... bumping into each other. I came up with a lot of witty remarks... after he had passed. Actually I was doing pretty good. He could only come up with "How are the toes?" and smile. Oh the smile, it was lethal.

Things came to a head two weeks after Paris' comments. Actually once again it was because of her that my life was about to change. You see, she had decided that an assistant designer should not live at the fabulous Times Square Motor Hotel. I must admit I was making enough to afford a better place. I may as well be completely honest, I was afraid with things going so well, something was bound to happen.

Paris knew this and felt no compassion for me. I had to endure a rather stern lecture on trusting God and myself, being positive and going for the dream I had been entrusted with.

After this I began looking for an apartment. My attitude wasn't entirely positive I must admit. I just figured I may as well enjoy life while it was good. Not exactly what Paris was trying to get across I know.

Anyhow, I was standing reading the community bulletin board. You could always find things there; a student wanting to sell used textbooks, even students looking for a roommate. It was while reading such notices that I felt someone come up behind me.

Without looking back I moved so that they could see and I could still read. They didn't quite get the idea, for they moved behind me again and continued to read over my shoulder. One notice caught my attention. I started to write down the telephone number given when my shadow spoke.

"Bad idea, her last roommate left because the rats and cockroaches started having gang wars." I glanced over my shoulder and was assaulted by those green-grey peepers only two inches away. "No kidding... well, maybe a little bit. The girl does not believe in cleaning." All I could do was nod. "Apartment hunting huh?"

No, I'm just reading the wall so I can write a book report. Trevor began laughing. I had only thought that thought... hadn't I? "That was good. I was wondering if you had a voice." I lost it just that fast. "Look, I know a place that's for rent."

"Really?"

"Yes really. I could show it to you tomorrow."

"You could?"

"Sure. If you trust yourself with me." I was not about to touch that one. Actually I didn't have to for along came Christy.

Christy was the picture of the proverbial California girl. Slim, no hips, blonde hair, blue-blue eyes, legs that started at her shoulders. Get the picture? Thought you would.

"Trev, I've been trying to catch up with you."

It as time for me to exit, unfortunately my self-appointed shadow had turned into my siamese twin or either AT & T. Every time I went to move away he would reach out and touch. At first I wondered if he was even aware of what he was doing, he was listening so intently to Christy.

I figured it was just reflex on his part, so I made a bolder move. Either he had a serious reflex problem or he didn't want me to go anywhere. I found myself pressed against his side, his arm around my waist and a hand on my hip to anchor me there. I was not about to try to move again. There was no telling what our next position would be.

Looking slightly over my shoulder I could see that California Christy was none too pleased. As her voice droned on I tried to remind myself to breathe. It was a test because being that close to Trevor was to say the least, disturbing. I knew I had to concentrate on something else or I would embarrass myself. Christy provided me with something.

"So, will I see you tomorrow? You know the entire gang misses you. It's been forever since we've seen you."

"Sorry Chris, we have plans for tomorrow."

It took me a second to catch on. When Trevor tightened his hold on my waist and pulled me closer, I was so um... moved, I almost missed the hiss that came from Christy. Almost. That was when I realized I was a part of that we. I must say an arctic wind would have been warmer than her voice.

Speaking of her voice, Christy has a way of talking which is unbelievable. She is a whiner. To give you an audio point of reference, do you know how Keith Sweat sung? Well, no matter what the song, it sounded like he was either begging or whining, that's Christy. Now add a few dozen layers of ice on that and you now have how she sounded at that moment.

"Well, I'm certain it won't take all day. I'm sure she has... something to do."

Now look, I am an easy going type of person most of the time. Except when I'm rubbed the wrong way and believe me, California Christy had rubbed wrong. Being of average looks, I can be sensitive. One of the things I can not tolerate is an ice-coated, superior attitude adjustment needed blonde, blue eyed whiner.

"Actually we'll probably need most of the night too for what we have planned." I could hear her teeth grind. I could feel Trevor shaking. Glancing up I could see the laughter reflected in his eyes.

"Yeah, we'll be going now Chris. I have to see Heart home so she can.... rest up." I could hear the laughter in his voice. Unfortunately Christy, well lets just say from the sounds of her heels tapping on the hallway floor, she didn't find the humor. "You are priceless." The laughter flowed out and I found myself pressed up fully against Trevor's chest.

Peeping over his shoulder I became aware of looks coming our way. I had forgotten we were in a school corridor. I groaned and momentarily buried my head in his shoulder. I guess my squealing didn't help to draw attention from us, but what would you have done had warm lips kissed your unprepared neck? The teddy bear hug didn't help either.

"Come on, I'll walk you home."

I was glad to get out of the building. I was also glad it was Friday, that gave me three days before I would have to face anyone again. I felt I was going to need that time to forget that scene.

I don't remember much about the trip to the hotel except that I was in no way cold. I believe I was given a kiss. I'm not certain because I was rather floating by the time I reached the room.

It was time for a reality check courtesy of one Paris. "Well, you've caught the boy, now what are you going to do with him?" That was my Paris.

I'm not certain what woke me the following morning, the telephone or the smell of breakfast. Still half sleep, I picked up the phone, you see punching it hadn't shut it off. "Hello."

"So, that's what you sound like first thing in the morning, not bad." One eye opened. "How do you look?" Now both eyes were open. "I'll be over in forty-five minutes, you don't have to get up, maybe I'll join you." We're talking wide awake now. "See you. By the way, good morning." I still held the phone as I listened to Trevor laugh before hanging up. It wasn't until the dial tone started buzzing in my ear that I realized I had to put it back on its base.

I was showered and dressed in twenty minutes. Mind you not because I believed Trevor would carry through with his... statement. Standing at the window, a cup of cinnamon tea in my hand I was startled when the knock came. Glancing around I noticed for the first time that while I had been daydreaming Paris had gone out. Sighing, I went to open the door.

"I don't like this. Do you know anyone can just walk in here? They don't ask questions."

"Good morning to you too." It didn't work. Trevor was upset and my humor was wasted.

"Get your coat, the sooner we get you out of here the better."

"May I finish my tea?" I found myself relieved of the half-filled cup. I watched fascinated in spite of myself as while watching me over the brim, he drained the cup.

"It's finished, lets go." What can I say, I went.

As it turned out, we didn't get to see the apartment. The agent called and I scheduled an appointment for the following monday. I figured my lunch hour would give me enough time to see the place.

Instead of going back to the hotel, I found myself at Trevor's. Now he lived at Lincoln Square, which if you know New York is as different from Times Square as bologna is from steak. I was starting to wonder if this was an ordinary guy.

He wasn't. After looking around his apartment and listening to what he didn't say, I found out he was one of those child genius'. In other words, mega brains. His knowledge of computers and business made me feel rather dumb. But his sense of humor made me feel warm. A bad combination. Learning that he had a weakness for old movies put the lid on my coffin. I was hooked. Seeing him cry at the end of The Way We Were nailed that lid shut. I was in love.

The day was filled with old movies, warm laughter and hot pizza. I had no doubt I was in love when I realized I was eating pizza with mushrooms. When I was a child I couldn't figure out how people could tell the difference between edible mushrooms and the poisonous ones so I would never eat any, just in case someone made a mistake.

Later that night, Trevor walked me back to the hotel. It was a nice distance but for me it wasn't far enough. At my room door he stopped. I found myself agreeing to go to church with him the next day. I must admit, when I said my prayers that night , (I had began praying again), I asked the Lord to help me to keep my mind on the service. I wasn't certain I could do it myself with Trevor seated beside me.

I was up early the next morning. I wanted to look perfect, well at least nice. I tried to get Paris to go with me. It bothered me that though my life was going so well I was seeing less and less of her.

"The Lord and I get together everyday. We're no strangers. You go and get reacquainted with him."

Once more she left before Trevor arrived. I had intended to tell him about her but it completely flew out of my mind when I opened the door and saw him. If you think everyday Trevor was something, Sunday Trevor was something else. This guy practically glowed. As I locked the door behind us, I asked the Lord to please remember what I had prayed the night before.

Just before walking into the church, I realized I didn't know what type of church I was about to attend. Now I don't knock anyone's religion but I find the entire thing confusing. The way I see it, if we all serve God, why can't we all serve him together?

Less than five minutes after entering the doors I found I needn't have worried. Make that five seconds. It's hard to worry when you're being hugged. I had never been hugged by so many strangers in my life. I was to find this was not the end.

I remember only a few words to the song every one sung. They were: Come in stranger, go out friend. I felt as though I had come home. Once the congregation was seated, I could feel what I can only describe as a presence. I glanced around and noticed Aja and her family. She turned and smiled from across the room at me.

I could feel anticipation in the air. I agreed with the pastor when he announced he didn't know what was going to happen. I could feel the presence building. Let me tell you, with what happened next, I needn't have been concerned about Trevor sitting beside me. The way things went, it was rather difficult to enjoy and lust at the same time.

The pastor began to speak, then he stopped. The entire congregation as one held it's breath. "Angels". One word. there had to be more, I found myself sitting up straighter. "Do not forget to entertain strangers, for by so doing some people have entertained angels without knowing." He appeared to look directly at me. Something jumped within.

As the service continued, the only way I can describe it is with a line from a poem: I put out my hand and touched the face of God. Sometime later I became aware of arms around me. Aja was hugging me. The service was over. I heard her whisper, "Welcome home."

I became aware of Trevor watching me. I was drawn forward to greet Aja's husband Samon and their daughter Sam. Watching them I could understand why they had fought to remain together. After many more hugs, Trevor and I were escorted out by their family. Once on the sidewalk we were asked to join them for dinner. I was not allowed to speak as Trevor accepted for the both of us. Inwardly I groaned at the sight of Aja and Samon's smile. I made a mental note to let them know Trevor and I were only friends.

The evening was filled with much laughter. I was delighted at another look inside my mentor's family life. To me she had it all. While in the kitchen helping with the meal, she gave me what she considered the secret of her success. "I pray, do my best and leave the rest to the Lord." It sound pretty easy. "It's not always easy and I mess up an awful lot, but it helps to know that even when I've missed it, I can go to him and say, well Father I blew it. And He forgives me. I try not to let it happen often but no matter how many times it does He's there and still loves me."

It really gave me something to think about. You see, I always thought that once you came to know the Lord, the mistakes and slips stopped. I'm certain we all know some holier-than-thou people who never appear to make any mistakes. As Aja said, "I would hate to be around when the sheets are pulled back on them."

We agreed to go back together to the concert that night. As it turned out, the morning service had been the meal, the night service was a very rich dessert.

The day came to an end with Trevor seeing me to my room. Knowing that Samon was waiting to take him home, I knew our goodbye would be short. It was. "See you at school tomorrow night friend." I was given a chaste kiss on the forehead.

Opening my room door , I watched him walk away. Closing the same door, I leaned against it and closed my eyes. The day had been unforgettable. "It was a good one."

Just like Paris, not a question, just a simple statement. I proceeded to tell her everything, trying to get her to see what I had experienced. "Oh I wish you had been there."

"I was dear, I was."

At the time I didn't pay much attention to that statement. I would recall it sometime later. That night I didn't spend a extended amount of time on my knees, instead I found it easier to lay down and talk to the Lord one-on-one. More as I would a loving father. For me it worked.

The next day bought some interesting developments. At lunch I told Aja of my appointment to see an apartment. As I prepared to leave she came to me. "Tina take whatever time you need. I'm sure you'll more than make it up later." I could see she wanted to say more but changed her mind. Instead she smiled and told me to get going.

"The rent would be two-fifty." I couldn't believe how calmly the woman sat. Of course I tried not to allow her to see that I was the extreme opposite.

"A week?" To myself I sounded like a mouse, an undersized one at that.

"A week... no dear, a month." Now I knew the woman had taken one valium too many.

"Two-fifty a month. For a split-level condo in the theater district?" I was waiting for someone to jump out and tell me I was on The New Candid Camera.

"It's not the way it sounds. You see, there will be a second tenant once one is approved. Really you are only renting one floor and until the second person moves in, you will be paying all the utilities. As you can see it balances out."

In my desperate state, I grabbed it. I just prayed it wasn't one of those too-good-to-be-true deals. Two hours later I was still walking around in a daze. I found myself with a key chain in my hand. Attached to the chain were two keys, one to the front security door of the building and the other to the condo, number 4/5A.

In my pocket was a Chase Manhattan savings ledger. It was the first time I had ever heard of paying your rent into a savings account but at this point not too much would surprise me. It seemed the owner of the condo was out of the country so they leased it rather than having it remain empty. They really didn't need the money, so they left it to sit in an account and collect interest. I still could not understand why the account was in my name as well as theirs. Then again how else could I make a deposit? At least that was what I told myself.

Anyhow, back to the condo. It was definitely the realization of a dream for me. Picture this: The bottom floor. You walk in the front door, three steps down is a sunken living room decorated in white and gold with black accents. Three steps up is a dining room, blue-black with gold accents. Against the wall, gold, brass and glass shelves. Did I mention the eighteen foot ceiling? I didn't think so, how about windows which reached from ceiling to floor? Big enough huh? I wasn't even concerned with having to wash them. Especially upon seeing the panoramic view. All this glass over looked the harbor. I didn't have to pretend I had a view while actually looking at the back of another building. This time I had one... really.

The kitchen was... a kitchen. No more hot plates. A chef's block sat in the middle of the floor. Get this, double ovens, Jeni-Air stove even. No more peanut butter and jelly, well maybe a little bit. I even had a mini-washroom with a compact washer and dryer. I had been informed if I wanted I could have it moved to a room outside the apartment so that it wouldn't bother me with noise while it was running. I must admit, I almost lost it when I was informed of that. Oh how the rich are different.

There was also a bedroom, nothing unusual, just a wall of closets, a waterbed and a full bath. No big deal. Right. Before I continue, that's right, that is not all. I was informed that until another occupant was found I had use of the entire place. Once that person was found I could take my choice of whether I wanted the top or bottom floor.

Okay, now go with me up the spiral stairs to the second floor. That's right, spiral. Here we find another bedroom, it's a dream, at least my dream. One wall has mirrored walk-in closets. Another is floor to ceiling book shelves. Oh the joy of filling those spaces. As you have come to expect, another large window over looking the water.

Once more there is a full size bathroom. Please note the double shell-shaped sinks and the large gilded hotel suite size mirror. I thought you would like that. Now outside the bathroom there is a cast iron ladder. I was informed it could be used as another bookcase. What it was for though was to reach the storage space located above the bedroom. Well after the agent left I went up to look at this storage space. Forgive my ignorance, but it looked like a loft to me. I don't know anyone who has a carpeted storage room with a half bath and a window seat.

The way I saw it, a silk room divider against the wall and voila, another bedroom. I mean even the storage room had bookcases. A hotplate and a microwave added and I would rent it. It was larger than my hotel room. Nicer too.

Not bad for two hundred and fifty dollars a month huh? Did I mention there is a mini-kitchen on the second floor? It's like having two apartments. The only inconvenience was that if I chose the second floor, I would have to go through the hallway to do laundry, pretty sad huh? It even had it's own door. The top floor was 5A, the bottom was 4A. Pretty nice. Now can you see why I was in a daze? I thought so. Who could have foreseen them turning an old National Guard Armory building into living quarters such as those.

By the time I made it back to the office I just knew Gabriel was saying to God, "Whew! She sure is making up for lost time. Boy can she talk."

The afternoon flew by, before I knew it, it was time to go. I decided to stop and see Aja. It was as though she had been waiting. "How was it?" She asked and boy did I tell her. As I talked, she smiled. After I ran out of words she started to laugh.

"Wow, I knew it would be special, he hasn't failed yet." I just stared. "We were praying for an apartment for you." I stared harder. "None of us liked the place you were staying in. The address is pretty bad. We knew the Lord would work it out and how!"

You could say that again. Later as I prepared for school, I told Paris about our new place. At least I tried to. After describing everything, I turned to her only to find her fast asleep. Before leaving I kissed her cheek and promised to tell her when I got back. Whispering, "I love you Paris," I let myself out the room.

One of the first people I saw that night was Trevor. I guess the foot long smile I wore told its own story, along with the hug I gave him. He promised to come over and help me move the next evening.

Entering the hotel later that night, I felt a coldness come over me. The place didn't look very inviting. Shivering slightly I let myself into the room. It felt glum. I can't explain it but I knew on the inside something was different, something had changed.

Glancing around, I saw it. On my pillow was an envelope. I didn't want to open it. Slowly I locked the door. Without reading what was inside, I knew. Paris was gone. My vision blurred as the burning tears came. Much later I was composed enough to read her letter.

> Well love, It is time. Have to go. Move on. God is watching, I am too. You'll make mistakes but you will make it. Be happy. Always remember the beauty.
>
> Love, Paris

Short and sweet just like the lady herself. I cried myself to sleep asking the Lord to take care and watch over her.

It didn't take any time at all for me to settle into the new apartment, though it had lost some of its pull without Paris. My life settled into a comfortable pattern. Work and school. My friendship with Aja's family and Trevor had deepened. Still it was as though a light had gone out. I was missing Paris. I hadn't realized just how much having her there had meant to me.

By this time a few months had passed. I had met a number of people at work, church and school, yet I felt lonely. I found myself watching couples. Envying them their togetherness.

While visiting Trevor one weekend, things came to a head. We had just returned to his apartment after seeing a late night double feature: Sabrina and Funny Face. Both starring Audrey Hepburn, both having fashion related importance. Both also about an ordinary girl finding love. In that was the danger.

A rather strange sensation came over me. It was as though I were standing back and watching a play unfold. I heard myself speak, but it was as though I were just a casual observer. Everything was really happening to someone else. I could just imagine how it would read in one of my favorite novels.

"I'm so sick and tired of being everyone's friend or sister. Just once why can't I be that someone special?" Heartina turned from Trevor, hugging herself. "Just once," she whispered, "I would like to feel that plain as

I am, I'm special to someone. Someone who will hold me, kiss me and make me feel desirable..."

Trevor came up behind her. Gently he wrapped his arms around her, holding her against his chest. One arm around her waist and the other across her chest. Heartina tried to swallow her pain. "I-I'm sorry..."

"Sh-h-h." He turned her into his arms and held her tighter.

Timidly, she placed her arms around his waist seeking a moments comfort.

"I..."

Once more he stopped her, this time by raising her chin. Heartina would not look at Trevor, not wanting to see pity in his eyes. Her breath caught in her throat as his lips gently touched her own.

Shocked, she moved to step back only to have his arms tighten and his head lower once again. The kiss which followed left her shaking and still trying to catch her breath. Dimly she became aware that he had not been untouched by the passion of their kiss as she felt a hardness against her.

Without a word, he led her to the bedroom. Once more he turned her to face him in the half light. With gentle hands he unbuttoned her shirt and slipped it down her arms. Heart racing, but afraid to speak for fear that he would stop, she ran her hands under his sweatshirt.

Her eyes flew open as he groaned at her touch. Impatiently, he drew his shirt over his head and flung it away. Startled at his almost violent action, she stepped back only to come up against the bed.

Trevor moved up to her again. Watching her, he unfastened her pants, hooking his thumbs into the waistband of her pants and panties. With one movement he drew both down her hips. With a gentle nudge of his head, Heartina found herself seated on the bed's edge.

Going on his knees as though uncovering something precious, Trevor drew her pants down her legs. He paused to remove her loafers, an instant later she was free of clothing as he ran kisses up her legs. She reached out to stop him as he kissed her inner thigh.

Raising his head, he leaned forward and placed a kiss in the valley between her breast. He stood, reaching down he picked up her hands. He guided them to his own waistband.

Taking a shaky breath, she unsnapped his jeans, with trembling fingers she unzipped and parted the time worn fabric. When her hands paused, he placed his own over them. Holding them trapped, he eased the material down his narrow hips.

Heartina drew back as his manhood was uncovered. Trevor allowed her to escape temporarily as he disposed of the remainder of his clothing.

Placing a hand on each side of her hips, he began to kiss her once again while pressing her back until she was laying down. With patient hands he repositioned her on the bed, then covered her with his body.

Heartina arched as does a cat when stroked as Trevor's hands journeyed over her heated flesh. His warm mouth replaced his hand on her breast. Leisurely his tongue circled the peaks, moving back and forth between the two as his hands roamed over her ribs and below.

She felt as though she were being consumed. So caught up in the unfamiliar sensations his touch was creating, she was unable to comprehend his question which was whispered brokenly. "Is it all right?" Watching her gazed over eyes, He withdrew from her. She mumbled a protest as his weight lifted. "It's okay." In a moment he was back, she had recovered enough to realize he had only meant to protect them.

This time, there was no hesitation as his leg nudged hers apart. Drinking from her parted lips, he caught her breath in his mouth as he entered her warmth. For a moment all was till except for their racing hearts. Then Trevor began to move with Heartina taking up the rhythm.

So intense the pleasure, Heartina felt the darkness drawing her. Not only did she find she could not see but neither could she hear. It was as though she had been wrapped in a warm cocoon.

She did not come out of this state until she felt Trevor withdraw from her. With his withdrawal, all of her insecurities returned. Turning on her side away from him, she did not se him throw an object into the trash can. Eyes closed to hold back tears, she tensed when she felt kisses being pressed against her moist skin, starting at her exposed neck and moving down her spine.

Heartina's heart leaped as Trevor turned her to face him and drew her against his chest. His gentle hands caressed her wet cheeks, yet he did not speak. She raised her head for his kiss. Grateful for his silence, she drew back and allowed her hands to travel over his face. Kissing his chin, she shifted until she was inclined over him. Slowly, using her hands and mouth, she mapped out a trail.

As her tongue circled his male nipples, Trevor seized her shoulders. She raised her head and watched him in the semi-darkness. Aware of his hardness against her buttocks as she straddled his waist, she began to roll her hips, not stopping when she heard his sharp intake of breath.

Trevor's hands slid to her waist and he shifted until he was impaled in her once more. This time he was in control. Almost savagely he pushed upward.

In an instant Heartina found herself on her back. As Trevor thrust into her, she drove him on with her hands pressing him closer. As the pressure built, she wrapped her legs around his waist. She met his every thrust with a wildness of her own.

The explosion when it came consumed them both. This time as they came down from the mountain Trevor did not withdraw. Wrapping her securely in his arms, they drifted off to sleep.

Heartina was the first to awaken. For a moment, she relaxed in Trevor's arms. Her eyes flew open as she remembered what had happened. Holding her breath she slowly detached herself from him. After quickly dressing, she stood over the still sleeping form.

Heartina allowed her eyes to roam over the tousled reddish-blonde hair, her hand itching to tangle in it once again. Her lips ached to once more trail over his warm skin. She covered her mouth as a small sob escaped. What had she done to their friendship? Pain raced her as she turned and fled the apartment.

Blinking, I found myself on the sidewalk. Dazed, I glanced up at the building behind me. It had been no dream, no book I had read, it had really happened. At that moment I did the only thing I could... I ran.

To say I was shocked at my actions would be a major understatement. A few hours later I heard the buzzer ring, followed by Trevor's voice. "Heartina, open up. Come on, we have to talk." I sat frozen, afraid to move for fear he would hear. "Heartina... please. Honey come on." Moments passed then I heard him mumble and release the button. Sinking to the floor, I cried and rocked, wishing Paris was with me.

When I woke up, I was still on the floor, but I was now covered with a blanket. Sitting up I looked around. I saw a silhouette, blinking I called out. The figure stepped into the light. Crying out, I came to my feet as fast as my cramped legs would allow.

I clung to Paris the way s frightened child would a beloved parent. I never questioned how she had come to be there, I only cared that when I needed her she had come.

I told her everything, of the pain, the loneliness and Trevor, leaving nothing out and never once thinking to lie or hide any part. "You did rather jump the gun." Without asking I knew she spoke of my night with Trevor. "Well, chin up, it's done. You can't take it back."

That was my Paris. A woman of few words. I had just returned from washing my tear stained face when the telephone rang. "Answer it."

I did. "Tina, we were wondering where you were. Trevor's here and he's frantic. Are you all right?"

"I'm fine Aja, I fell asleep."

"Trevor told us about... the two of you. Don't be upset, he was worried about you."

"It's okay, I'm okay. Tell him..." I wasn't allowed to finish because Trevor came on the line.

"Heart, are you okay?"

"Yes Trevor, I'm..."

"Where are you? I came looking for you."

"I..."

"We need to talk."

"It's all right..."

"I'll be over." He hung up before I could agree or disagree.

I turned to Paris. "What am I going to do or say?"

"Follow your heart."

"It's not my heart I'm afraid of." I mumbled. "You're not leaving again are you Paris?"

"I have to."

"Why? I don't understand."

"You will."

"When?"

"Soon."

Well, I got through that meeting with Trevor though I didn't remember how. In the month which followed, I came to know even more about him. I had never known why he was at the college. It seemed three nights a week he helped with the computer classes. I found this out the second semester when I had to take one.

It was pretty hard to concentrate with him around for three hours walking around the room and looking over your shoulder. I must be honest, as an instructor he was hard but fair. Mid-semester, the regular instructor returned.

We still managed to see each other on a regular basis. With all the walking we did, I started to lose weight. It helped that I was once again missing Paris. Therefore I was skipping meals and going to bed rather than spending a lot of time in my own company.

So there I was, my life well rounded. Now I had a best friend, nice job and fine home, my prayer life was even better. As things go I was overdue I guess for some type of snag. Trevor and I had started going to the fitness center. He felt being that I kept complaining about my figure, I should do something about whatever I had complaints about.

I knew he was special when I found myself talking about my thunder thighs around him. It was after a vigorous work-out session that we returned to my place to shower. Things were not the way they may sound. Remember I had two bathrooms.

Being that we had planned to go to the movies, we decided it would be better for him to get ready at my place rather than go to his then have to come back for me. After showering, I found out just how vigorous our workout had been. Laying across the bed, I found I couldn't move.

Later, when Trevor knocked on the bedroom door, I was still unable to move.

"Tired?"

I groaned.

"Sore?"

I groaned.

"No movie?"

I groaned louder.

"How about a massage?"

I sighed. Feeling bone tired, I faintly felt him peel back my robe. I groaned as he lifted my arms to remove them from the sleeves. As his hands began to massage my sore neck muscles, my brain turned off. I began to dream.

When he straddled her at the waist, she caught her breath. Feeling the heat of his thighs against her ribs, his smooth buttocks against her rear end, and a hardness nudging against the small of her back, all tiredness fled only to be replaced by an aching need.

"Um, maybe this wasn't such a good idea after all."

"No?"

"No. I feel fine. I'm not tired any more."

"You're not?"

"Nope, not at all."

"Good." His weight shifted as he turned her over beneath him. "I'm so glad."

When his mouth covered her own, Heartina's groan was swallowed before it could surface. Slowly his tongue stroked the inside of her mouth, then imitating a more intimate act, he began to thrust deeper and deeper, his tongue used as a rapier.

Hold it, time out! This was no dream. Once again I found myself in a position I didn't want to be in. All right, so that was stretching the truth a bit. I mean I shouldn't have wanted to be there. Being friends is more important than being lovers... right? Well, at the time my hormones would not have agreed.

I tried to come up with an innovative way to stop things, which was pretty hard when you're skin to skin. My reasoning sounded pretty good. I only had one slight problem... my body wouldn't respond to my brain or at least the half that was trying to be loyal. The other half was having a ball, where my body and senses were the guests of honor.

Bet you know what happened next huh? Bet you don't. Obviously while I was being controlled by raging hormones, Trevor was a different story. "Marry me." I don't know where that came from but wherever it came from there was another one behind it. "Marry me."

Raging hormones became somewhat controllable. "What?" Was that my voice sounding husky and weak?

"Marry me Heartina." Trevor drew back.

"Uh... can't we just be friends?" I could feel myself blushing as he pointedly looked down at our entwined bodies. I tried again. "Good friends?" Boy did I blow it.

"That's usually what men say to women and I think they're fools to go for it. I never thought I would be in that position. Well, there's only one response. If you want to bed me, you'll have to wed me."

Man, where did he come from? "Trevor..."

"One answer Tina. No jokes, yes or no?"

I could not believe the position I was in. I felt if I were to say "yes", the dream would end and I would wake up. If I said "no", I would have my dream turn into a nightmare. I opted for something safe. "Can't we talk about it later?"

Silence. Things were still quite an hour later as I sat on the bed watching television, or I should say it watched me. You see, Trevor decided we could talk about it later... much later. He left. I tell you, that's a guaranteed way to cool hormones down real fast.

This time Paris didn't show. Instead, Aja came over. I didn't even get a chance to say anything. She took one look at me and made a simple statement. "It's better to marry than to burn."

Tonight for the first time, I dined with Trevor's family. It wasn't at all like Guess Who's Coming To Dinner. After dinner, we moved to the family room. In the hallway I noticed a portrait. Under it was an engraved name plate which read: Paris Ane L'Anglais.

For a moment I gazed up into the face I had come to love. I felt Trevor come up behind me. I leaned against him as he spoke in my ear. "That was my favorite grandmother. I can remember her promising to find me the perfect wife." He raised my left hand and kissed the wedding band on my finger. "Had she lived, I'm certain she would have come up with you."

I felt as though I had been surrounded by a sunbeam. As Trevor led me to the room in which his family waited, I glanced back over my shoulder. The portrait seemed to glow with warmth and the smile was as mischievous as I had come to expect. I smiled back and heard my heart whisper, "Paris, you old... angel."

Beast Of Burden

Denice heard the music playing softly in the background. She didn't want to return to the party, she couldn't return, not just yet she thought. She gave a tear drenched laugh as she noticed the words to the song drifting upon the night air.

> I can't take it no more,
> I'm gonna knock on your door
> 'say why won't you notice me...

At the chorus, she closed her eyes.

> 'Cause I'm alone in this world
> And I'm in love with you girl.
> Can't you see, oh won't you please
> notice me...

If only, she thought. If only there was a seed of truth on your part Miles, just one grain of feeling. With head bowed and her thoughts in turmoil Denice was unaware of the glass door which separated the balcony from the dining room being opened. Nor was she aware of the figure which approached on silent feet.

Not until hands descended on her shoulders was she aware of no longer being alone. Slowly she turned. Her breath caught in her throat as she glanced up and saw the face before her. It seemed as though she ceased to breathe as that face lowered until Miles' lips covered her own.

Faintly she felt herself being pressed against the rail, but the feel of being wrapped tightly in Miles' arms overshadowed that slight discomfort.

WANTED: Single female to take part in scientific experiment for period of three months. Non-smoker, non-drinker. No drug user need apply. For more information, call (213) 4A-ANGEL.

I wonder what that's all about? Denice thought to herself. Glancing at the clock above the refrigerator, she threw down the newspaper she held and headed for the door.

WANTED: Single female to share two bedroom, two bath condo. Rooms with a view. Beverly Hills area. Mansion available on weekends for three months. CALL (213) 4A-ANGEL.

What a dream. Denice sighed. Slowly, she allowed her gaze to wander around her cramp studio apartment. To be able to live like that. Rising slowly, she gathered her purse and tote. Taking the time to refold the newspaper, she gave it a wistful pat before she turned and headed out the door.

"Denice, where are you?"

Denice smiled and glanced up. Peering over the shelves she spotted the source of the voice. "Over here Faytra, by the stockroom."

"Did you see it?"

"See what?"

"The ad for the condo and the mansion. Sounds nice."

"How much?"

"It doesn't say."

"It's too much."

"How do you know that without calling?"

"Because it doesn't say."

"All right... so when are you going to call?"

"Tomorrow." Both began to laugh.

"Did you see it?"

"See what?"

"The new ad?"

"There's another one?"

"Figures... look."

Denice took the slip of paper Faytra handed her. The girls were on break together. This marks the third day the ads had appeared, each one more unbelievable than the last.

> *WANTED: Single female for scientific experiment, period of three months. Rent paid for six months plus monthly allowance five hundred dollars. All expenses paid. CALL (213) 4A-ANGEL.*

"Wow, I wonder what kind of experiment? It's probably dangerous or either it's not legit."

"Why don't you call and see? It may be all right."

"In that case Faytra why don't you call?"

"Well, it says single female."

"You're single, well at least for the next six months." At her friends' expression, Denice smiled. "Well maybe not six whole months."

"Denice..."

"Okay, come on. I'll call. It's only a quarter, what can it hurt?"

"So what did they say?"

"Just enough to set up an appointment for me to stop by tomorrow during lunch to talk."

"What's the experiment?"

"I don't know but I think it has something to do with psychology."

"That's great. It won't take three months."

"Huh?"

"They'll find out you're crazy the first day and that'll be it. The easiest five hundred dollars you've ever made." Faytra ducked to avoid being hit by the flying purse.

"Miss Jackson, be honest with me; how do you feel about the proposition I have just made to you?"

Denice looked at the woman seated behind the desk. "I feel... as though I've just stepped into the twilight zone."

"If you accept I warn you, there may be times when you feel as though you're in a certain other place. But I assure you it will be well worth your while if you stick with the program."

"Three months?"

"You did what?" Faytra stared at Denice as though she had lost her senses. Indeed Denice felt at that moment as though she had.

"I signed the contract."

"You signed a contract? Let me get this right. You signed a legal contract giving someone you've never seen before three months of total control over you? Niecey, I though I was kidding when I said you were crazy, now I'm not so sure you aren't."

"Join the club. One minute we were talking and the next I was signing. Maybe it won't be so bad. I survived the army didn't I?"

"I wonder if all of you made it after all." Faytra looked skeptical. "When does this... experiment start?" Denice began to fidget in her seat. "You haven't told me everything." Faytra closed her eyes, "Spill it."

Not looking at her, Denice took a deep breath. "I can't work."

Faytra's eyes opened, "Huh?"

"I can't start until I've quit work."

"Right, now why didn't I know that?"

"Faytra, they are paying my rent and I get five hundred dollars a month. I won't have to buy or pay anything for three months. That's not bad... I don't think."

"Exactly, you didn't think! What if it's like being in prison? Why would anyone want to totally control someone else anyhow? Oh boy, this is going to be something else." Faytra dropped her head to the table at which they sat. "Lord please help your child."

"I'm going to need it." Denice added.

"Well, maybe ninety days will go by fast. Maybe you'll survive." Faytra mumbled, head still on the table. "Denice only you could get yourself in a mess like this."

"You said it."

"Well, they say God looks after babies and fools." Faytra peeked at Denice.

"Enough already, I get your drift." Denice groaned and her head joined her friends' on the table.

"Well Denice how do you like your gilded prison?" Minutes passed as Denice tried to think of words to describe all she had seen and all she felt at that moment. Never before had she been privilege to be in a place such as she now found herself. All she could manage was to look at the woman seated across from her and shrug her shoulders. "How do you feel honey?"

"As though...as though I'm in a dream. A very pleasant dream and I'm about to wake up at any moment."

"Well dear it's going to go on for a bit longer than a moment. By the way, my name is O'Keefden, you can call me Storm though." At Denice's expression she laughed. "I was named after the weather. My mother loved storms, she said it was the only time nature could rage and get back at man for all he does to her. Now tell me what you think; about the house, not storms." She smiled.

"The house, what I've seen of it is beautiful. As for the bedroom, it's rather odd."

"Why odd?"

"It's the bedroom of my dreams, well the bedroom I've seen in my dreams. I can't explain it but it's as though I've seen it before."

"In your dreams why were you here?"

"I don't know, I believe I lived here."

"Was there anyone else here with you?" At this question Storm leaned forward as though expecting some vital bit of information.

"I can't remember." Denice felt as though she had somehow disappointed her.

"That's all right. Now tell me, how do you see yourself?"

"What?"

"Forget that question. Tell me, if you could change anything about yourself, what would it be?"

Denice laughed. "How long do we have for me to tell you all?"

"It can't be that many things."

"Don't bet on it."

"Then just tell me five things to begin with. What do you think are the most important, the most vital?"

"To begin with..." A far away look came into Denice's eyes as she leaned back in the high-back chain in which she sat. So caught up in her mustering was she, she did not see the slight nod Storm gave to the silent figure in the doorway.

"Miles are you certain you know what you're doing?"

"Yes auntie."

"I mean it. She's a very nice girl. A bit world-weary but very sweet."

"I'll handle her like a child, Storm."

"That may be the problem." Storm stared at the young man who now occupied the chair Denice had been seated in only an hour before."

"Don't worry so much, it's just an experiment. No one will be hurt. I'll have my completed thesis and she will have had an experience she can look back on and tell her children about." Miles stood, leaning over he kissed his aunt. "It's only for three short months. What could happen in that time? Goodnight, I have a busy day planned for tomorrow."

After he had left the room, Storm answered his question. "In three months you could find yourself with the perfect woman for you and have to let her go."

Denice groped for the telephone. "Rise and shine sleepy head. It's time to set the gears in motion. We'll see you in the dining room in twenty minutes."

Before she could speak the connection was broken. She laid back into the pillows. Suddenly her eyes flew open. "We? Who is we?" In a single movement the covers were thrown back and she was sitting up. An instant later she was standing. "And who was he?"

"Less than fifteen minutes, that's pretty good." Denice stared at the man seated at the table.

"Come on in honey. You have to eat breakfast before you and Miles take off. Come on, step to it." This Storm added when Denice remained standing in the doorway.

"Miles?" Slowly she advanced and seated herself in the space Storm indicated.

"Yes, my nephew Miles. He's the one conducting this experiment. It's for his master thesis. I'm very proud of him."

"I just bet you are." Denice thought, peeking across the table at the nephew.

"Eat." The vision spoke. "We have a busy day ahead. You will be needing the energy."

And what a vision he was. His chiselled features alone could inspire poetry. But no, that was not enough. His hair was to be envied by man or woman. Full and wavy it hung golden brown slightly beyond his shoulders. The eyes Denice, what about the eyes?

"Denice?"

Denice was startled at hearing her name. "I'm sorry, what did you say?"

"I said I know what you must be feeling."

"I hope not." She mumbled under her breath.

"Pardon?"

"Nothing."

Storm smiled and Denice felt the color wash over her cheeks. Quickly she ducked her head and began to study the bran muffin which sat before her. "I know it's a shock to find out Miles is the one who's conducting this experiment and not I. I hope you forgive us for the deception. We wanted to make certain we had the right person."

"Do you? Do you have the right person?"

"I'm positive we do. Aren't you Miles?"

"Positive," he looked directly at Denice for the first time," absolutely perfect."

"Brown, liquid brown." Denice glanced down again, embarrassed that she had spoken her thoughts.

"What?" Miles questioned, looking slightly puzzled. Storm began to laugh and Denice blushed even more.

"I'll pull out his hair and scratch his eyes out. Well maybe I'll just run over him with this bike gently, then have him stuffed." Denice mumbled to herself.

The vision had turned into a nightmare. For three weeks she had endured what she considered cruel and unjust torture. For three weeks she had been forced to physically exert herself more than she had in her entire twenty-five years.

It had started out nice and simple. Miles had taken her shopping. Storm had gone along. Denice had found herself fitted with every type exercise shoe available. In three weeks she had used every pair... twice.

Now she sat, well not actually sat, more like slumped on the stationary exercise bike. She had just been granted a five minute break. Weary, she allowed her eyes to roam over her own personal torture chamber as she had begun to call Miles' exercise room.

And how dare he look so good, she scowled; for dressed in shorts and a next to nothing tee shirt, he looked very good indeed. Even at a time such as this she had to admit he was indeed a fine specimen. At six feet two, not a spare ounce of flesh dared park on his sculptured body.

"He even sweats sexy." She mumbled. This thought caused her to scowl even more.

"Wipe that look off or he'll know he's getting to you." Denice didn't bother to change her expression as she turned her head to take in the cool picture Storm made in her strawberry and white sweatsuit, minus the sweat.

"Every time something starts becoming easier to me he changes to something else." She emphasized "he".

Storm studied the younger woman. Indeed there had been times when she questioned the pace Miles had set for Denice but now, even in her exhausted state, she smiled slightly, and mad state, she could see the massive results. Storm doubted if even Miles or Denice herself had taken the time to notice what special changes had taken place.

Miles with his scientific notions and schedules, Denice with her fiery determination not to allow him to get the best of her or make her give up, had together worked a small miracle in that short span of time.

The two were interrupted by Miles' approach. "Okay ladies, if the chat is over we can start again."

"Miles," noting Denice's rebellious expression, Storm intervened. "How about making that enough for today?"

"Storm, I..." he started to interrupt.

"She needs rest for tomorrow. I insist." Storm's voice left no room for disagreement.

"Go ahead Denice, relax, be ready at five tomorrow and in the living room." With those instructions, he turned and stormed out the room, anger apparent in every line of his body.

Denice started to speak but was halted. "He'll get over it. Go shower and relax. I'll have dinner sent up to your room. Go on, I'll be up later to see you." She patted her on the shoulder then headed after her nephew.

"Why did you interfere?" Miles moved around the room like a caged lion ready to strike.

He is magnificent, Storm thought as she watched him; but for now she had to think of what was at hand. "Miles, she's not a machine. The child was exhausted."

"You're interfering with my project auntie."

"Your project is a human being. For three weeks I have kept silent as I've watched you push that girl to her limits. I have watched her go beyond and do so much more than anyone should have to do in this short span of time. What are you trying to do to her? What are you trying to achieve? Do you even know any more?"

Miles stopped pacing and sat down. "Oh tante," with head back and eyes closed he didn't see the warm look Storm gave him at the use of his childhood name for her. "She has so much potential. She's capable of so much. So much that's been wasted."

"And after you use it up what then?" He opened his eyes and looked at her. "What will you do after you've awakened everything in her, given her new dreams, new desires? What happens at the end of three months? Will she be thrown back into the world she came from with half fed desires? A cruel world that doesn't care how it crushes her dreams?"

Miles tried to protest but he was not allowed the chance to speak. "How will she be able to maintain what she's had here? Do you really want to take the responsibility for giving her dreams just so the world can take them away from her?" Storm rose and walked to the study door, opening it she turned. "What are you going to do with the woman you've awakened? Think about it, think about it very carefully." With this final warning, she walked out closing the door softly behind her.

"What does he want from me Storm? I give it my all and still it's not enough. I can never please him. Just when I think I have he turns and gives me another set of instructions. It's as though he can't bear the thought of my succeeding. Why?"

The woman watched the girl seated on the bed. She noted the tears still clinging to her lashes though she had wiped them from her cheeks before answering Storm's knock. She also saw the trembling mouth. She felt the urge to take Denice in her arms, and she did. "It's a test of endurance. It's to see how fast a person can adjust to changing environments."

"And he wants me to fail. That's why he tries to make it so hard." Denice mumbled against Storm's shoulder.

"Hang in there baby." It was the only response Storm could give.

Denice raised her head. "I won't let him beat me." She vowed.

"That's my girl. It's time my beloved nephew found out things don't always go as planned."

"I'll be strong, " Denice placed her head on Storm's shoulder, "tomorrow".

Gently, Storm rocked the young woman in her arms and smiled.

"We can rest for awhile." Miles stopped and started to lower his pack to the ground.

"How much farther to the sight?"

"Four or five miles."

Then lets keep going." Not looking at him, Denice continued to walk, following the trail they had been following.

Miles watched her for a moment then slowly settled his pack once again upon his back. During the three hour drive and five hour hike, he had noticed subtle changes in Denice. Not once during the hike had she asked him to slow down or to stop. During their brief rests she had paid no attention to him whatsoever. He had to admit that this factor in itself had served as cause for him to watch her more closely.

In all honesty, he had grown accustom to her sneaking looks at him when she thought herself unobserved. It served to flatter him greatly. Now, over night it was as though she could no longer bear the sight of him. He lengthened his stride to catch up with the rapidly disappearing figure ahead of him.

"We can camp here. Rest for awhile then we'll set up the tents." Miles sat down after placing his pack against a boulder. For a moment Denice stood glancing around. An instant later she walked over to a spot under a tree, knelt and began to unpack her pack. "What are you doing?"

"I'm putting up my tent." She answered without glancing up.

"Rest, then..." He was not allowed to finish.

"You can rest." She carried on with what she was doing.

Silently Miles watched. He had to admit it was rather delightful to watch her movements. In just over three weeks Denice had indeed changed. Her movements were more sure. He confidence was growing. Once again he heard his aunt's warning issued before he had left that morning. "One day you're going to wake up and realize she's more than just a means to finish your thesis. You'll realize she's a woman, then what are you going to do?" That day had arrived.

Denice wiped the tears from her cheeks. "You seem to be doing that a lot lately,' she whispered to herself. Slowly she stretched her aching back. Actually she thought, everything she had ached. She was so tired she didn't think she would be able to rise from where she kneeled. "But I will get up. I have to." She spoke softly.

They had set up camp and built a fire. They had eaten in silence. After a quick walk around the surrounding area, Miles had announced it was time to turn in for the night. Determined not to allow him to see her pain, Denice had told him to go on and turn in. She gathered the plates and utensils they had used and moved to the small stream they had discovered in their walk to wash them.

With head bowed to her task, she waited for the sounds of Miles' entering his tent. Only then did she allow her body to sag. Rising slowly, painfully, she staggered to where her own tent was pitched. Biting back the cry which rose to her lips as she bent down, she entered, allowing the flap to fall into place behind her.

Quietly Miles allowed the flap he held still to part. For a long time he had watched Denice. He wanted to go to her for he had seen her pain, but he knew at that moment she would not welcome his seeing her weakness. After a time, he allowed his own flap to close. Miles laid awake in the darkness.

"I don't understand it tante, she wouldn't even let me help her. I knew she was tired but she wouldn't even let me offer her a hand. Why?"

Once again Denice had gone to bed and Storm and Miles were in the study. Storm watched her nephew pacing the floor. "Why would she turn on me like that?" His brows knitted together, he continued without waiting for an answer. "She wouldn't even slow down. Why has she changed?"

"Isn't this what you wanted? Aren't these the results you were hoping for? She's adjust to the point where she's strong enough to handle and endure without your help. She doesn't need your support. Isn't that what you wanted?"

"No. Yes. I don't know exactly what I wanted." He stopped his pacing and sat down, head in his hands. Storm leaned forward to catch his mumbled reply. "I just know this isn't it. This isn't it." She thoughtfully studied his bowed head.

Denice slowly shifted over onto her back. With sleep-filled eyes, she looked up. Miles stood at the side of the bed watching her. "What is it?" She asked softly.

"Just making certain you're resting."

"What about you?"

"I'll be fine. No turn back." This was spoken to halt her move to turn on her side towards him.

"But I..."

"Sh-h-h," he hushed her, "slide over."

Without thought her sleep drenched mind had her obeying. She felt the cool night air caress her back before being replaced by the warmth of Miles' body as he laid beside her. Gently wrapped in his arms he drew her against his length. She felt a gentle kiss on the nape of her neck, then warm breath as she heard him whisper, "Go back to sleep. I'm just going to hold you."

As trusting as a child, Denice did as he said, quickly surrendering to love-washed dreams.

"It was only a dream."

"You sound disappointed, besides, are you certain it was just a dream?" Faytra watched Denice across the restaurant table.

"I'm positive. I'm only an experiment to Miles. No feelings attached."

Faytra noticed the slight slump of her friends' shoulders. For the past half hour, Denice had brought her up to date on all which had happened in the past thirty days. "So what happens now?"

"We start phase two."

"What is that?"

"I don't know. I'm never told anything ahead of time."

Faytra could feel her pain. "Niecey, be careful," she pleaded, "be very careful."

"It's too late Faytra...it's too late."

"So what do you ladies think?" Four faces peered in the large salon mirror.

"It"s..."

"Wow!"

"It's..."

"It's you Denice, definitely you."

"Hi me."

All four started laughing. "Jerome you've done it again. It's perfect."

"Thanks Ms O'Keefden. It's easy when you have something this good to work with." The young man smiled at Denice through the mirror as he gave her hair an extra fluff.

"If Jerome has finished we can get on with our plans." Miles had walked over to the group. After speaking he turned abruptly away. Faytra and Denice exchanged puzzled glances. Storm and Jerome exchanged smiles.

Denice flinched as the study door slammed shut. Looking slightly ashamed she faced Storm and Faytra. Storm was the first to break the silence. "Miles is in a fine temper. What happened?"

"Suzanne Liverwurst." Denice glared as she spoke the name.

"That's Lillyfoot, which is just as bad but go on."

"Well she kept on and on about how she missed Miles and how she would be so relieved when his experiment was over. Every time she came near me she would throw cutting and degrading remarks at me."

"And..."

"Marina Cavoso finally asked her what was the problem with her being civil." Here Denice stopped and studied the rug on which she stood.

"And..."

"I hadn't realized how quite it had become..."

"So..."

"So Miles came up and she all but melted into him." Storm smiled at the distasteful expression on the younger woman's face. "He asked what was going on, and... I said... nothing a good laxative couldn't cure."

"And everyone heard." Faytra concluded.

"And everyone heard." Faytra and Storm roared with laughter as Denice stood staring at her feet blushing.

"Miles, the child didn't mean to embarrass you. Denice wouldn't..."

"Denice?" He looked at his aunt. "Denice behaved, I have to admit, better than I would have had the situation been reversed."

"Then why are you angry at her?"

"I'm not angry at her. It's Suzanne. How dare she pull a stunt like that!"

"Did you tell her?"

"I most certainly did after I had put Denice in the car."

"I meant did you tell Denice it wasn't her you were angry with?"

"Why would she think I was angry with her?" At his aunt's expression, Miles closed his eyes and groaned.

Denice felt the mattress dip as another body joined her in the bed. Turning, she felt strong arms reaching for her through the darkness. Gently she was drawn to Miles' chest and soft, warm kisses were placed on first her forehead then eyes and nose. With barely a pause her lips were taken in a long, warm, moist, deep kiss. Slowly, their lips parted.

"Why do you only come in my dreams?" Denice whispered, placing her head on Miles' chest.

For a moment he did not respond. Holding her tighter he raised his head to look into her sleep-filled eyes. "Would you like for this to be real?"

Closing her eyes, she snuggled closer. "Very much so," he heard her whisper before completely surrendering to sleep. For some time he laid in the darkness gazing at the ceiling, yet not seeing it. The first rays of morning were crossing the sky when he finally moved to gently detangle himself from Denice's arms. Before leaving, he placed a final kiss on her lips. His expression was tender and very thoughtful.

"I don't understand the two of you." Faytra marveled at what Denice was telling her. Once again they were having lunch together as had become their habit in the second month of the great experiment. "You argued over a car?"

"Faytra, I didn't need a car. The bus was just fine."

"The man bought you a car."

"He keeps buying me things."

"And you're complaining?" Faytra shook her head in disbelief.

"I don't know what he's going to do next. It doesn't take all of this. I mean the man gets angry because I hadn't been using the car, does that sound normal to you?" Faytra was silent. "Well?"

Faytra smiled. "I can't wait to see what he does next. This is better than television." She caught the napkin thrown at her.

"It's a what and we're going where?" Denice couldn't believe what she was hearing. "Once again this is a credit card for your use and come on. We're headed for Paris." Storm headed for the door. "Come on child, the plane is not going to wait." She sighed, recrossing the room, she grabbed a shocked Denice by the arm and pulled her behind her.

"What did I do this time?"

"Denice, you know Miles doesn't like it when... you attract attention."

"But Storm, we were only talking about places the guys could see when they go to the states. I wasn't embarrassing him." Denice paced the hotel room as she spoke. "Is there no way to please him?"

"Baby..." She was not allowed to continue.

"I would think that he would be happy to know I can adjust to a new environment. Isn't that what this experiment is all about? Why else would he teach me French and bring me to France?"

"I think it's time we had a little talk. Miles..." Once more Storm was interrupted, this time by a knock at the door. She sighed. "We'll have to finish this later."

"Enough already. I've had enough!" Denice swung around to confront Miles. "Every since this thing started I've put up with your moods. Everything you've ordered, I've tried to do. But I have had enough. I refuse to allow you to intimidate me any longer. I don't care who you are, I've done nothing wrong. There were no rules which said I couldn't dance with anyone."

"You call that dancing? He was all over you, I don't know how you could even breath you were so close." Miles vented his own anger.

"We were a respectable distance apart. And anyhow, it was none of your business."

"It's my business because I brought you here," he turned his back to her, "it's disgusting how you were practically making love in the garden."

"What!" She screamed. "It was one lousy kiss. One kiss doesn't mean a thing now days!" She walked up to

---

him and grabbed his arm. "And don't turn your back on me!"

Miles swiftly turned, startling her into stepping back. "One lousy kiss? Doesn't mean anything? Well how's this for nothing?" He stepped forward and seized Denice by the arms. Dragging her the short distance to his chest, he lowered his head and seized her lips with his own.

The kiss which started out hard and angry, soon changed into one which was long, deep, warm, moist and slow, as to appear to go on for days. It was also heavily flavored with longing. It ended only when it became necessary for them to breath once more.

Breathing hard, they drew apart. Moments passed as they stood staring at each other. Neither spoke. "Am I interrupting anything?" Storm poked her head around the room door. Seeing the two avoid looking at each other, she knew she had.

"Hey girl you made it, three whole months." Faytra approached Denice in the kitchen.

"Yeah, I made it. It's all over." She didn't sound happy.

"Does he know?" She wouldn't look at her friend. "Does he know you love him?"

"It was only an experiment."

"What about the kiss?"

"That was a month ago, it was probably forgotten by the next day if not sooner."

"On his part."

Denice sighed, "On his part."

"No one kisses anyone like that without feeling something."

"He was angry and probably thought it best to kiss me than to hit me."

"Right. I go around kissing every one I get angry with too."

"Lets just drop it. This is a celebration. We are here to celebrate that Mr. Miles O'Keefden has finished and turned in his thesis for his Masters. Let's join the party now in progress." Denice laughed dryly and headed for the living room. Faytra was slower to follow.

With head bowed and her thoughts in turmoil, Denice was unaware of the glass door which separated the balcony from the dining room being opened. Nor was she aware of the figure which approached on silent feet. Not until hands descended on her shoulders was she aware of no longer being alone. Slowly she turned. Her breath caught in her throat as she glanced up and saw the face before her. It seemed as though she ceased to breathe as that face lowered until Miles' lips covered her own.

Faintly she felt herself being pressed against the rail of the balcony, but the feel of being wrapped tightly in his arms overshadowed that slight discomfort.

"Another experiment Miles?" The moment was shattered by the intrusion of a male voice.

Denice pulled out of Miles' arms. "Excuse me." Without looking at either man, she moved inside.

"Are you sure Denice?"

"I'm sure Faytra."

But there's another three months on your contract. You get to stay in the mansion three months after the experiment."

"I wouldn't be able to. I've had more than enough. I'm certain no one will protest."

"You should at least say goodbye."

"I'll leave him the car keys and everything else he brought, maybe he can return most of it."

"Where are you going?"

"Probably visiting or something." Catching the look on her friends' face, she added. "Faytra, promise me you won't tell Miles I'm leaving." At the look of guilt she knew she had guessed her intentions correctly. "Promise me." She insisted. Reluctantly, Faytra promised. As soon as Denice had left the apartment, Faytra looked for Storm with a gleam in her eye.

The pain inside was so intense, Denice made not a sound as she laid on the bed crying. "Lord, please hold my heart, it's breaking into a million pieces. Please hold my heart." She cried. "My fault, my fault. It was only an experiment. But Lord the pain, I can't take the pain."

So deep her misery, so violent her pain, Denice was unaware of anything around her. With eyes closed, she was locked in a world of torment. She was unable to hear the voice of hope or to see the light of truth. Locked into the darkness and pain which sought to engulf her, she did not see the figure which had been standing in the darkened corner approach her. Nor did she feel the weight which settled on the bed beside her. She was unaware of the gentle hand which wiped away the tears falling from her eyes.

Ever so faintly, hope and truth merged until they were able to pierce the darkness which was her pain. As the pain began to rescind, she could feel the prayers of her friend reaching out to her. With a heart wrenching sob, she opened her eyes. Not a word was spoken as Miles watched her. After a moment, he spoke quietly. "This is no dream. They never were."

"What do you want?" Denice whispered.

"Female needed for lifetime experiment. Experience necessary." As the two embraced, they were unaware of the other two presences in the room with them.

"Well Agilire, we can go. They're strong enough to hold on to each other now."

"For a moment there I was concerned." Agilire glanced at Tratoc, "But only for a moment."

In an instant the two unfurled their wings and sailed up through the ceiling and into the sky above on their way to another field to other lost sheep. They went drawing them together for their master the Great Shepherd.

The Gift

My fiancee' was the picture of the handsome groom; his bride was also lovely in my wedding gown. Had I but known the type day the day before my wedding would be, I believe I would have overslept.

I arrived at the rehearsal to be greeted by my fiancee's nervous brother. He informed me with sweat running in rivers down his face that Lathine needed desperately to see me in the changing room. I went forward with great eagerness.

You would have to know my Lathine to understand my eagerness. You see, Lathine and I grew up together. We were best friends from the age of eighteen months, therefore it was rather expected that we would eventually get married... to each other. We had in all our years of growing, never found anyone who could take the others place, therefore on my twenty-eighth birthday, Lathine proposed.

His proposal had not come as a shock to anyone much less myself. We had always been together except for that one summer he chose to travel to California. I would have been with him then had not my uncle Herman decided to take a walk one night... off the pier. Lathine and uncle Herman never got along very well. It was neither of their faults actually. Uncle Herman was just very protective of his favorite niece... me. For some strange reason he had this ridiculous notion that Lathine would some day hurt me, he was absolutely convinced and would not be shaken.

Well, on this day I hurried to rendezvous with Lathine, you see, the night before we had discovered a new avenue in our relationship, it was called passion. It had only taken one unexpected kiss and an entirely new dimension had been added. We had always been confidants, friends, partners but knew not of the scope of passion we were each capable of together.

As I hurried down to the church basement, I can almost remember the tune which was playing in my head. Almost. I entered the room seeking my prince, instead I found myself faced with a frog. Very politely, being forever the perfect gentleman, Lathine unwrapped his arms from around the body of the woman standing before him who was not me. He was even nice enough to remove his lips from her own.

As I stood there swaying in no breeze, I calmly was informed that he would indeed be getting married the next day... only not to me. You see, that summer had brought about more than just a severe case of sunburn for Lathine, it had brought about Sheila.

In terms which even a child could understand if they listened, I was asked to do just that, understand. Lathine and Sheila had fallen in love that summer and couldn't get up. As it so happened, Lathine had been unable to do anything about it because of a slight problem... fear of her husband. But as in all fairy tales, she had arrived in town early that morning... divorced.

The pair was so sweet in asking for forgiveness, adding the fact that our pastor had just arrived, I found myself graciously forgiving them both. For who can win against love? My forgiveness was so complete that I offered to give Sheila my wedding gown, she already had my husband-to-be. I figured she could use the entire package. It wasn't as though I had any immediate use for it.

The wedding went on as planned, only in a country town can one phone call prepare everyone for such a change in less than twenty four hours... I hate the country. The entire town turned out for the wedding... savages, traitors. There was only one moment of discomfort, that was when I entered and they could not decide which side to seat me on, as friend of the bride or groom. My mother tells me I was very brave... and very stupid. Actually I was replaying past episodes of Murder, She Wrote in my mind.

After the brief service, which ended with everyone saying what a beautiful couple they made and how they knew I would always see that the right thing was done, I even offered to drive the happy couple to their new home; the apartment Lathine and I had so painstakingly remodeled and decorated. There was yet another surprise waiting for me. Lucky me. I was asked that being the swell sport I was if I would mind taking Ginger out for awhile. Of course I said yes. No one would possibly spend much time investigating the sudden demise of a pet I figured. Besides, I couldn't see where I could be made to feel any lower, I was wrong. You see, Ginger was not the family pet but rather the daughter they had created that summer long ago... together. This Ginger was a beautiful seven year old.

As it were, I kept Ginger for a whole week in order to allow the newlyweds a honeymoon. The day I returned Ginger was the day I moved out of town. The move was accomplished rather quickly for I found it easy to pack when everything which can be broken... is.

Two years later there was a knock at my door. A door located in a different state. I opened it to find Lathine, Sheila and Ginger on my doorstep. I was again asked to take care of Ginger so that the two of them could enjoy some time alone. Of course I intended to decline, that was until I looked at her, you see that week two years prior had been a very hard time for me. I had fallen in love with little Ginger, totally against my will and superior judgement.

Two weeks later, the happy couple returned for my Ginger. My mother swears to this day she knew my life would never be the same for she claims it was at that point that little Ginger began to look like me. I heard nothing from them until three years later. I was once again in a different state. I have yet to learn how they learned my new address but my mother always did have a rather sly smile.

This time they were having problems in their marriage and wanted me to watch Ginger for an extended period of time. I was not to know how extended. A month later I received a packet in the mail. In all honestly I was not the least bit alarmed by the big brown envelope... until I opened it. There was a brief letter letting me know they would be out of the country for awhile and knew I wouldn't mind watching the child. Enclosed were all kinds of legal papers I would need to enter her in school or anything else I could come up with. In polite terms, for the duration she was mine.

For six glorious months I complained to my mother about the gall of the two then hung up afterwards and enjoyed myself with Ginger. Then something even stranger happened. I began to dread every time the phone rang or the doorbell sounded. For a brief time, we considered taking an unscheduled trip to the Bermuda Triangle, leaving the return date open... indefinitely. Only our mutual dislike for flying insects which bite brought us to our senses.

One day, nine months later, I received a phone call from what's-his-name and his wife's lawyer. He wanted to see us the next day, he said he had a very important letter for us. We agreed on a time to meet. I was sorely tempted to accidently miss the appointment, I did not give in. Ginger and I willed ourselves to be brave. Two hours before the meeting we cried in separate rooms. We did not want to be parted. We even discussed demanding visitation rights. It was only when I reminded myself Ginger was Lathine and Sheila's daughter that this idea was dropped.

High noon arrived as did the lawyer. Ginger and I swore to keep a stiff upper lip. The moment the doorbell sounded, two bottom lips hit the floor.

Sometime later the lawyer, such a nice man, had gone and we sat dazed on the sofa staring blankly at each other. I felt very bad and repented within for the delight I had taken in imagining the two had some how met with a terrible accident which left them not dead exactly but rather unable to take Ginger from me. You see, there was no need for that, she was now legally mine for better or worst. I knew it was going to be a breeze for we had been through worst already. Lathine and Sheila had decided to stay away, they had given me complete custody. May they have a long life. They had decided having a child was a great inconvience to their way of life. I also realized that from that moment forth the law would have something to say should I ever decide I wanted to send my little gift back.

I am now a single parent and I find I love every moment of it, with the exception of those moments when darling Ginger starts to act like... me. You-know-who gave me a wonderful gift of freedom and self when he decided to marry what's-her-name.

Ginger is now fifteen, she is graduating from high school today, number one in her class. My baby is growing up and looking just like me, her mama. Just think, I have all of this and didn't even have to sweat and suffer birth pains. When pregnant women ask me how much my baby weighed when she came I just smile as I tell them the truth... fifty-two pounds, and she came gift wrapped.

Lightning Source UK Ltd.
Milton Keynes UK
UKOW02n0840151214

243137UK00001B/2/P